BREAKING
SMITH'S
QUARTER
HORSE

PAUL ST. PIERRE

Douglas & McIntyre
Vancouver/Toronto

Douglas & McIntyre Ltd., 1615 Venables Street,
Vancouver, British Columbia V5L 2H1

Canadian Cataloguing in Publication Data

St. Pierre, Paul, 1923-
Breaking Smith's quarter horse

Originally published: Toronto: Ryerson
Press, 1966.

ISBN 0-88894-431-4
I. Title.
PS8537.A54B7 1984 C813'.54 C84-091077-0
PR9199.3.S24B7 1984

Cover photographs by Stephen Bosch
Cover design by Barbara Hodgson
Printed and bound in Canada by D. W. Friesen & Sons Ltd.

Preface

If there is a moral in this book, it is not my fault. If there is social relevance, it crept in without alerting me, in which case I would have hit it with a stick. This is a story, nothing more. I make no apologies for calling it just a story. In my view, the only reason for writing a book is to tell a story.

Story telling is an old and honourable trade. The first stories were told around camp fires and the last will be told there too. They were told for people seeking to entertain themselves by examining the almost limitless varieties of the human animal. A story made some sort of order of men's affairs, but not too much. After all, luck arranges much of what we do and forces called fate, destiny or the devil do their share too. Most men who tell stories do not pretend to excessive understanding of what happens in them.

There are other conventions. Typically, the past is a part of every story. Invited or not, it was there. Sometimes, in a story, men think they can also catch a glimpse of the future, but of that they can never be sure.

The language by which a tale is told has always been very important, but no one has ever been able to say precisely why. Possibly it is because language, English and all the others, is almost as imperfect, irrational and variable as man himself.

Many stories, some good, have been told in cow camps. *Breaking Smith's Quarter Horse* is one of that strain. It has been around now for one generation of man so perhaps it deserves some examination (although not too much). It appeared first on CBC television in the 1950s under the title "How to Break a Quarter Horse." The odd horse trainer watched that show in hope of improving his style, and was cruelly disappointed. It appeared again on television in the early Sixties. In 1966 it appeared in book form, published by an Eastern outfit whom I shall, in a ridiculous excess of kindness, refrain from naming. Disney Studios bought the rights and used them to create a movie called Smith. I was never responsible for that Smith. Those who did not like him may apply to Hollywood for relief from their suffering. There have also been large numbers of high school and college students who have been told to read the quarter horse story and don't ask why, because it's part of the curriculum, that's why. I feel sympathy for these young people — it is hard to listen to a story for no other reason than that it is supposed to be good for you. I never read a book for such a reason. However, students from time to time brought me comfort, as when a Grade 10 pupil in Hamilton, Ontario, wrote his appreciation of the book: "It was pretty boring, but at least it was better that Shakespeare."

Now, *Breaking Smith's Quarter Horse* appears again in this new edition by Douglas and McIntyre. Nothing in the original text has been changed. It has all its warts. I would have liked to improve it, for the failures of telling that story are all too apparent to me today. But publishing tradition says you can't go back again. I guess I will go along with tradition. However I shall here use a few lines to reflect on the long life of Smith and his quarter horse, of Norah, Ol Antoine, Gabriel, the Judge, and the rest of them. Why have they and their story endured? Why is there a not inconsiderable number of readers who seem to understand these people, understand them, possibly, better than I did myself when I first wrote of them. Belatedly, I find myself looking for the reason. That reason must be in the people of Chilcotin, who made this book.

I have written about that country and those people since. Now and then I am asked why. Who could be interested in such people when there are captains and kings who are obviously of so much more importance in our world? Have I been deprived of elitist company and if so why haven't I applied to Canada Council for a grant so that I might mingle with the great? I have not been deprived. Life has dealt me pretty good cards and I have been privileged to associate with politicians, newspaper publishers, policemen, diplomats and, of more *gravitas* than all the others, bureaucrats of the mandarin class.

Why not, then, write about these movers and shakers of society? There is a reason, although it has taken some years for my conscious mind to catch up with what my subconscious had earlier recognized. Most of the people of high degree in this world whom I have met simply weren't as interesting as the ranchers, cowboys and Indians of Chilcotin. The expense account society looms high on the close horizon of the public prints, but its people tend to be nervous and uncertain men, more concerned about what others think of them than of what they think of themselves. More often than not they are, truth to tell, a bit dull. If you write about dull people you will write a dull book.

The Chilcotin people have many faults, far more than I have space here to mention. But they know who they are. They know what they want to do. They know, even better, the many things they damned well won't do. Thus their lives are not frittered away in anxious examination of themselves, their works and their status. Like people anywhere, their lives are complex, sometimes sad, often foolish, occasionally tragic and now and then poor and mean. But never petty. They are people of whom it is said that they may be wrong but they are never in doubt.

Whether or not this book adequately portrays them is for the reader to say, not me. However, there are people who contributed much to the book and, without burdening them with responsibility for what I say, I would like to thank them for their help: Duane and Marian Witte of the Teepee Heart Ranch at Big Creek; the late Cecil Henry of the Bighorn Ranch at Big Creek; Judge Lee Skipp, formerly of Williams Lake; Norman Blake, who was Government Agent in that town, and rodeo cowboy George Palmantier, who is on the cover with a horse that is one quarter something in the breeding.

Above all I would like to acknowledge the wisdom and the perception of the late Mrs. Lester Dorsey of the Four Mile Ranch at Anahim Lake. Her name was Hannah but she went through most of her life with the nickname Mickey. She lived a life of hardship and danger and to her they were both just salt and pepper. If it were not for Mickey the story of breaking Smith's quarter horse would probably never have been told and a lot of people still wouldn't know how it was done.

January 2, 1984
Fort Langley

CONTENTS

Smith

To seek the beginnings of the story of the
breaking of Smith's quarter horse would take
too long. It might be impossible. Who could
say how far one might have to backtrack in time,
following the blood lines of quarter horse stock
and of Smiths?

For practical purposes, the final episode began
on a day in late January when Smith herded the
old range cow out of the timber and down the
buckbrush flat to his Home Place. Rider, horse
and cow came slowly down the long gap in the
pines, following the line of the Oregon Jim
Creek where, in summer, the black water from
Smith's swamp meadows leaked away towards
the Pacific Ocean a gallon at a time. Oregon Jim
Creek was now frozen solid, and so was Smith's
right ear. The sky had the hard luminosity
of a clean ball-bearing and the air had a dreadful stillness. When the sap in a jack pine
exploded a mile down the long meadow it
sounded as close as a shotgun going off fifty
yards away. There was every indication that the
night was going to be even colder than the one
before.

Sometimes in winter the cold air from the far north made a pool over the Namko Country. It drifted down slowly, a breath, a sigh, over the patchwork of meadows and pine and swamp and lake that lay just inside of the Coast Range. Then the land groaned as the weight of the cold settled upon it. Two days before there had been two sun dogs riding right and left of the pale sun. Within twenty-four hours the cold air had seeped down and on Puntlakuntlet Lake the two-foot-thick ice began to split in long, jagged, lightning-shaped cracks, with the appropriate noise of thunder. The previous night an old dog coyote had lain down and tucked his grey nose into his thin tail beside the Russel fence of Smith's Home Place and in the coldest hour, just before the dawn, he had died. Man is supposed to be the only animal who spends his adult life anticipating death but it would be easy to believe that the old coyote had some sense of the futility of it all when he had lain down in the poor light of a young moon that night.

The ravens were now at work upon the coyote's carcass, beginning with the eyes.

It was that kind of winter and that kind of day when Smith started thinking about the quarter horse again. Sometimes he thought about that horse because he saw it, sometimes he thought about it because he couldn't see it. On this day he couldn't see it. He could see a thin blue pencil mark of smoke pointing at the

2

chimney of his house, which was a small log cabin, and he could see the humped shoulders of a moose inside one of his hay corrals where it was eating hay much too expensive for moose. A dozen of his horses were pawing away two feet of crusted snow to get at the grass beside the creek. His Hereford breeding stock, which could no longer rustle their own feed, were moaning about it. Nevertheless he thought about the quarter horse and he said to himself that he was going to by God have the quarter horse broken the way he by God wanted it broken by Ol Antoine by God and that there was no two by God ways about it.

Smith was a very ordinary sort of man. He was in his late thirties at this time, smoked rollings, used the standard Association saddle and from the top of his head to his heels was one straight line, which some people say is a sign of stubbornness and others attribute to Irish ancestry. It is quite common among men who ride horses a lot. He had been born in the Thompson River country and his mother had died too early for him to remember her. His father was a Jack Mormon out of Utah who came to Canada in 1910 and died in '43 on a bet that he could swim his horse across the Skookumchuck.

Smith had come into the Namko Country to build a ranch on the four-thousand-foot contour of the fifty-third parallel of north latitude. One might say that he and men like him should have

3

more sense. One might be right. Indeed, in the current view of government and industry, such country is better left unsettled until such time as a large corporation is prepared to establish instant towns therein, complete with pre-sliced bread and dripless candles. Nevertheless Smith went there and tried to build up a ranch.

On those ranges, over the years, there had been many names. There had been Larsens and Zieleskis and Dilloughboys, there had been Johnsons and Roughton-Hensons and Saw-chucks and Pappajohns; there had been at least three Jack Macdonalds from Cape Breton. Some were dead and some were wiser and some still hacked it there. But it happened that in all that range there was only one Smith. He was the only Smith in all the Namko Country.

His closest approach to fame had occurred more than a decade before on the Ortona River in Italy, where he had served with the Loyal Edmonton Regiment. An Italian pig had become wounded in the course of that war. She lay between the lines, squealing, and it was Smith who took out a platoon to contest with members of the Hermann Goering Division in an effort to free that pig's suffering spirit into roasts and chops. Before the action was over it became necessary for the Canadians to lay down a full regimental artillery barrage in order to get Smith and his platoon and the deceased pig back to the lines, leaving one or two members of the Hermann Goering Division dead and

4

several others thoughtful. Stories getting distorted as they do in being relayed back to Main Div, there was talk for a while of giving Smith the Military Medal but after consideration they took his stripes away from him instead. This suited him just as well. He never wanted to be a sergeant in the first place.

His Christian names were common knowledge only to his banker, the Brands Inspector, people in the Grazing Division of the Forestry Department and a few others set in authority over him —people whom he disliked for that reason. He was known as Smith.

He had four sons whose names were Sherwood, Roosevelt, Exeter and John, his wife Norah having got to name one of them.

In addition to many horses, many many horses, many, many, many horses, he had a Border collie named Rappaport, called Rap'ort. When asked about the dog's unusual name Smith would sometimes tell about it. There was a cowboy who had a dog of that name. This cowboy became lost for many days in the N'miah country. After two weeks the cowboy found it necessary to eat Rappaport. As the cowboy was finishing up the last of the meat he said, sadly, "Poor Rap'ort, what a pity he isn't here. He would have enjoyed them bones."

On this day Smith rode an old Blue Roan. He had taken her on a bad debt from some Indians. She had been hard used and the white hairs of old saddle sores made the map of Mexico upon her back. She was ewe-necked and more than a little sickle-hocked. She had nothing except endurance, the quality that can never be sufficiently apparent to horse show judges.

The Hereford he herded down the big meadow at the Home Place was an old thing with no loin whatever, only bones. The cold that afternoon was twenty below or worse and it had apparently curdled her brains because she persisted in turning back towards the black hills of pine to bawl as if for a lost calf, despite the fact that she had been barren for three years and would never again bear a calf or use her horns to keep the coyotes away from the awkward little thing as it struggled up to its feet beside the black pool of the afterbirth.

In this way the three of them came down the long buckbrush flat, Smith, the Blue Roan and the old cow, and a reasonable man would say that if all three of them cashed in their chips that afternoon the destiny of the Canadian nation would not be altered by the breadth of one hair. But, what the hell, we all have to make a living.

Smith slipped the saddle off the Blue when he brought her into the yard, and kicked her in the guts as she tried to bite him, which was a bad habit she had, and then he walked on the creaking snow up to the house where his wife, Norah, had stood by the kitchen window watching him, getting madder by the moment, as he had come down the long flat.

It was a very ordinary house and it suited him very well. It was made of logs, chinked with a mixture of sawdust and flour paste. Originally it was a one-room cabin with a flat roof of layered sand, clay and sod, where flowers bloomed in early summer. As he had acquired wife and children he had extended the old Home Place, first by adding a T extension, then by building a pitched roof of hand-split shakes above the sod roof, then by enclosing the gabled ends of this attic to make upstairs bedrooms, then by adding a roofed porch where his wife sometimes succeeded in growing hops despite the bite of frosts that could occur in any month of the year.

Smith had also put a sink in the kitchen and had led a waste pipe through the log wall and towards a rock pit, but he had not yet connected this sink to the drainage pit. The sink drained into a five-gallon bucket, which was emptied from time to time by anybody who noticed— Norah.

They used coal oil lamps and gas lanterns. The toilet stood one hundred feet from the house and was made of logs, unchinked. It was the coldest place in all of Namko, possibly in all the world.

In the preceding summer Smith had built yet another line of his endless fencing between house and toilet. He had not yet found time to make a gate through this fence. The fence itself had required a month of hard work. The extra day needed to build a gate had not been found by him. No doubt there was such a day, but he had not found it.

Some of these features of the Home Place annoyed Norah, in a general way. On this day her annoyance was not general but specific. Smith had been away for two days and he had neglected to notify her when he was going, where, why, or when he might be expected to come home.

Norah

He kicked open the door and pulled off the old-fashioned buckle overshoes that he had worn over his moccasins. He hung his bat-wing chaps beside the door, put his hat on the peg, threw his mackinaw on the old sofa and slapped his APH pants and said, "Cold, ent it."

"Smith," she said, "where have you been?"

"Colder'n a witch's tit," he said, walking towards the kitchen stove and leaning over it. "I really do think, Norah, it is time we closed down the swimming pool for this winter."

"Where have you been?"

"Now, Norah, all is well. All is well, Norah."

Having been married to him for fourteen years, she stopped talking for a few minutes at this point and went to the stove to heat up the moose-meat stew and the coffee. Norah was a small woman with a snub-nosed face and hands so rough now that she sometimes cried about them. She was thirty-two and looked more. Her figure was still very good, the legs long and straight, the hips wide but with a smooth curl from the thighs outward and in again to the waist. Her breasts were rather small, but neat.

When she wanted to smile she could do it very well. Her taste in dresses, which she wore on the rare occasions when they went out to Williams Lake or to the Namko Stampede, ran a little towards the gaudy. Also, she was known to use four-letter language sometimes. But she had a strong sense of duty, which happens to be one of the things that distinguishes ladies from tramps.

She jammed new wood into the stove—it had never been big enough in the firebox to take it, but she jammed it in anyway—and while the stew began to bubble and Smith sat by the table, looking opaquely towards a feed-store catalogue that featured a large bull and a small man holding its halter, she began to talk again.

"All is well!" she said. "Damn it all, Smith, we are not gonna make it this winter."

He switched his attention to the Wing's Café calendar. That one showed a girl, slim, blonde, clad in high boots and thin underclothing. She was undressing beneath a purple waterfall amid some unusually high mountains. Yong Wing had arranged for this calendar to be sprinkled thickly with mica flakes so that it sparkled in the dim light and it certainly did catch a man's eye, over there beside the old escritoire under the sheep horns in the living-room.

"I have been out the last two mornings," she said, "forking out that hay to them poor creatures on the meadow. Those cattle are starving, Smith. That hay is rotten. Rotten. Rotten. They

10

would never choke it down except that they are starvin."

Smith said, "We can't be surprised about that. We knew it was smoking wet when we put it up last fall. We knew it would only make chewing tobacco for them."

"It's like feeding them snowballs."

"Yep, that's about it. Like feeding them snowballs. Well, maybe it will fool them. Maybe they will live until spring on love, like I been doing. Is that coffee ready yet?"

"And you, you crazy little bastard," she said, while pouring him coffee, "you take off in the middle of winter, twenty below or worse, and are gone two days without so much as a by-your-leave or see-you-next-Sunday."

"Well," he said, "when I was out feeding two mornings ago, I just took a notion that them three old cows we never got off the high range last fall might have held up on Long Opening. And it didn't feel too cold that morning, so I just took off, on that old Blue Roan."

"You rode up to the Long Opening, in this weather, dressed that way?"

"Well, I found them. All three of them there, politely starving themselves to death in three feet of snow."

"Oh, well," she said, "that's something. Three cows more than we thought we had."

While she dished out the stew and brought it over she thought some more and said, "You did get all three of them back?"

"As a matter of fact, no. Two of them was too far gone when I got there. I shot them right where I found them. But that other old cow looked a little more skookum so I broke a trail out for her and she followed me over Kappan Mountain, with the Blue Roan and me breaking through five feet of snow. This morning, after we'd camped, I hit the creek and we followed it down to here."

"And you froze that ear again," she said.

"It was a cold camp last night," he said.

Norah put her small red hand over his ear. "Did you rub snow on it?"

"That don't help. It will thaw. It always has."

She sighed. "It always has."

"Is there any katchup?" he said.

"Dear God," said Norah, "is this winter ever gonna end, Smith?"

"If it don't, I figure it will be the longest on record. Is there any katchup?"

"We are down to seventy-eight on the breeding stock, and you know that banker told you that even a hundred-cow ranch isn't at the break-even point any more."

"Well, then, I will have to eat it without katchup."

"And the hay is rotten. The smoke comes out when you lift it. And we had to start feeding before Christmas this year. Think about it, Smith. Before Christmas. They couldn't even rustle until Christmas this year."

12

"Either the moose of the Namko Country are gettin tougher or my teeth are gettin softer," he said, "because, katchup or no katchup, I can hardly chew the gravy of this old beast. Who killed this one, anyway? Was it Sherwood? He should have more sense than to kill a bull as old as this one."

"It was not Sherwood. As you know perfectly well he and Roosevelt have been out at the Lake since September, at the boarding school, where they are eating more than we are making right now on this ranch."

"Next year will be better," he said. "I am goin to do some trapping now and next fall there is six parties lined up for guiding. Where is Exeter and Johnnie?"

"We left Exeter at the Larsen's two weeks ago, to wait until the dental clinic came through at Arch MacGregor's store."

"Oh, yes, that's right."

"And John is asleep."

"Well, he has got the right idea. I think I will do a little of that myself. There is not enough sleeping done in this world. I was remarking on that point to the old Blue Roan last night when I had her tied up beside that big spruce where I slept." He crossed his forearms on the table and dropped his forehead upon them.

"Before you go to sleep you might as well know that there is something really serious going on," she said.

13

"Mmmm? More serious than starving out this winter?"

"Yes."

"Won't it wait until I close my eyes for twenty minutes here?"

"Oh, I spose so," she said. Although the kitchen was warm she put a light blanket over his shoulders and he slept, scarcely stirring, for almost an hour.

Ol Antoine

She fed young John his bottle and kept him quiet. From time to time she went to the window to peer out through a small hole burred through the frost that covered the panes. The cabin was beginning to creak in the chill of the gathering night when she spotted Ol Antoine coming up the path from the old soddie cabin. Then she reached the table in three long steps, put her face opposite his on the table and said in a tight and hard voice, "Smith!"

His head came up. He was instantly, fully awake. It was a peculiar ability of his that often startled her. Now, looking into his dark eyes, the pupil unclearly separated from the iris, the look flat and dull as a piece of cloth, she wondered again if there were Indian blood in Smith. So many of the old families had Indian blood.

He waited for her to speak.

"Ol Antoine is coming up here," she said. "He's been down in that old soddie cabin in the sidehill."

"Well, that is nothing to get excited about, except maybe for me, as he has finally come to

15

break that quarter horse for me, I spose. I was thinkin today that by God . . ."

She broke in. "Never mind about that stupid horse. I tell you I have been scared witless for two days."

"Scared? Of Ol Antoine?"

She lowered her voice. "There is somebody in there with him," she said.

"Aah," said Smith, speaking as one to whom all things have at last become clear, "someone with him. I tell you, it is a girl. That's what it is. It is a girl. It's a love nest he's got down there. Let me see now, how old is Ol Antoine? I once added up all the stories he's told about himself and I think it came out to one hundred and thirty-four—and that would be three years ago—so he'd be a hundred thirty-seven. . ."

"This is no joke, Smith, and it is no girl in that old soddie."

"Of course it is a girl, and a good thing, too. It is a great opportunity for me. Now, while he is inflamed with passion, at the age of a hundred and thirty-seven, now I am at last in a good position to make sure he finally does that job for me." He rose from the table. "Yes sir, he is going to do that job this year, and no mistake about it."

Before she could answer the door opened slowly and Ol Antoine said "Hello, this place."

"Why," said Smith, "if it ain't Ol Antoine. Klahowya, old man." He then turned to Norah and, speaking loudly, said, "It is the turn of the

16

Smith luck, Norah. This winter ain't gonna be known any more as the Smith Disaster. Ol Antoine has come to break that quarter horse for me."

The old man looked at him and then walked out of the kitchen, past the ladder-like stairs that led to the bedrooms and into the sitting-room. There he seated himself beside the drum heater. It was a small room, but it contained many deer horns, sheep horns, moose horns and guns; also reproductions of Remington and Russell prints; photographs of horses, home-made copper bas-reliefs of horses' heads, an escritoire jammed with unopened bills and unanswered letters, and a chesterfield and an arm chair with broken springs. Ol Antoine did not use a chair. He upended a piece of firewood and sat on it.

Smith leaned in the doorway, watching him and ignoring Norah, who was plucking at his sleeve. Smith liked to look at Ol Antoine. He could never fully understand what was in the old Indian's mind, and he respected that in any man.

Ol Antoine was an interesting sight, by normal standards. He had heaped upon himself all the thin clothing that he owned. His feet were in ankle-length moccasins, over which he had drawn thin dress rubbers. His pants were of heavy blue serge. They had been obtained somehow through a used clothing outlet and were now shiny with the fat of many beaver skinnings.

Ol Antoine's sweater had been knitted by a member of some women's auxiliary to something, possibly for the benefit of the troops at Sebastopol. On his head was a black hat, which he did not remove. Around his ears was wound a scarf. This old man was variously described as uncle, grandfather, great-grandfather and, of course, cousin by most of the Indians on the Namko Reserve. His true age was a matter of speculation, even for those interested enough to consider it. The first whites to take up land in the Namko Country remembered him as being exceptionally tall, but now he was less than five-five; the gristle separating his vertebrae had thinned and granulated, the normal S curve of the spine had become exaggerated and his head was now carried low on his thin neck. Some said Ol Antoine would never die, in the ordinary sense, but would one day just disappear in a puff of his own dust. He was a man possessed of many stories, rarely told. It was said that he claimed to have ridden with Chief Joseph of the Nez Percés when that nation fought the American cavalry regiments in its long and unsuccessful attempt to get over the Canadian border, seeking the haven that Canada had not long before given to Sitting Bull and his Sioux. It would be possible, were Ol Antoine over ninety now and under twenty during the Nez Percé war, that he did take part

18

in that sad campaign, but highly improbable. The Chilcotin language bears about as much relationship to the Nez Percés' as does Chinese to Dutch and in any case the Chilcotins were a lonely group of Indians who kept aloof from even the neighbouring Shuswap across the Fraser River.

They were a people noted for high cheekbones, wide mouths and sultry temperament. In 1864 they had carried out a small war against the whites. Their leader had been a big man with a wide mouth and hard mind whose name comes down as Klatsassan-Chilhoseltz. Klatsassan had blue eyes, which might be taken as a tribute to the warrior spirit of visiting Caucasians, although it is a curious fact that the first white man ever known to pass through the Chilcotin, Sir Alexander Mackenzie, noted in his diary that he was met by blue-eyed Indians somewhere south of the West Road River. Possibly Cossack blood from the Russian steppes had filtered through Alaska and into Chilcotin before Mackenzie's time.

The British Columbia colonial government had listed the uprising as a war, seeking to be repaid for the costs of its volunteer soldiers by the Colonial Office in London. This failed and the uprising later came to be called the Waddington Massacre and was dismissed from public notice as just another brawl. It was forgotten by almost everybody, except a few Chilcotins.

Ol Antoine claimed to have been a warrior

19

for the Chilcotins also, but then he claimed so many things.

The Chilcotins are the southernmost extension of the great mass of Athapaskan-speaking Indians who cover the north of Canada. Islands of people who speak a related language extend far to the south and into modern Mexico. In the United States the best-known members of this group are the Navahoes and Apaches, who were similarly dissatisfied when whites took their land away from them.

Interestingly enough, in the centre of the modern Navaho Reservation, north of Gallup, New Mexico, is a lonely butte, which geographers call Ship Rock but which is, according to Navaho legend, the Great Bird that brought their ancestors down from the north.

After killing a few whites and dodging two small white armies, Klatsassan and some of his fellows surrendered. The government temporarily suspended war status and treated them as murder suspects instead of as prisoners of war, and they went on trial before Mr. Justice Begbie.

(It might be said that their defence was conducted under some handicap, since the evidence of wild Indians was not then accepted in British Columbia courts. This, however, was later rectified and the present B.C. Evidence Act (Section 12, Chapter 134, Revised Statutes of British Columbia, 1960) provides that a judge may receive "evidence of any aboriginal native, or native of mixed blood of the continent of North America, or the islands adjacent thereto, being

20

an uncivilized person, destitute of knowledge of God and of any fixed and clear belief in religion or in a future state of rewards and punishments, without administering oath. . . .")

On October twenty-sixth that year Klatsassan, Taloot, Tapeet, Chessus and young Pierre were all taken out and hanged together at Quesnelmouth.

Klatsassan left few words and little mark upon his country. The only legend which comes down from that campaign is that when he surrendered in the expectation of pardon and was ordered to give up his musket he broke it against a tree instead and said, "King George man big liar." But there is no proof of this and it is believed, generally, only by the Chilcotins.

It was, in any event, of no concern to Smith on this cold evening. If he had ever heard such tales, they had failed to impress him. His only apparent interest on this day was the quarter horse, and he began by discussing that animal.

"It is maybe going to take us a day or two to round up that horse, Ol Antoine," he said. Ol Antoine did not answer.

Smith twisted a cigarette for the old man and continued speaking, gently, as he did so.

"I come all the way down the Home Place Meadow today without spotting him. He must be off with that half-wild bunch of mine that hang out on Happy Ann Meadow. We tried to bring him into the ranch yard so he might gentle up some but every time he went out right over the fence. He is like a deer now."

21

Ol Antoine spoke in his own language to an audience that one might judge to be larger and more distant than Smith. Smith touched his arm to restore Ol Antoine's attention and held the cigarette before him. Ol Antoine took it, held it between his thumb and middle finger, allowed Smith to light it for him and then, pushing his lips out to meet the cigarette as his hand brought it back towards his mouth, he puffed smoke rapidly without inhaling. He did not smoke often.

"You know, Ol Antoine, there are people who would say that you are a little bit late in breaking that horse for me, on account of that horse has now passed his sixth birthday and has never felt the touch of leather."

Ol Antoine lifted one arm and spoke slowly, but with feeling, to a band council or to some other group of people who understood Chilcotin.

"Who cares about that damn horse?" said Norah.

"I care," said Smith. "That is going to be a great horse. A really great horse."

"It is Bulldog Quarter Horse, and you know it. Look at how heavy them shoulders are, look at them pasterns, it'll have a trot that will jar your head off."

"It is not Bulldog Quarter Horse," said Smith, "and as for how it trots I am not planning to take a beef drive in with it, it is going to be a cutting horse. A really great cutting

22

horse. And it is gonna be broke in the old-time Indian way. Ent it, Ol Antoine?"

Ol Antoine did not reply but Smith did not mind. His ear had scarcely begun to pain yet. He lit his own twisting and blew fragrant blue smoke into the quiet air of the little living-room and he said in an easy voice, "A beautiful thing to see, how an Indian can talk to a horse. He never roughs him up. He never drives the irons into him. He just takes him out, after he gets a halter on him, and he talks to him. He has got just one turn of the halter rope around a snubbin post, like my finger there, and the Indian is on one side of the snubbin post and the horse is on the other side, and he just talks to him. Sometimes he spits in his face a little bit or he puffs his breath up into the horse's nostrils. Like this. *Puh. Puh.* That is the way he goes about it. A beautiful thing to see."

"I never saw any horse broke that way," she said.

"Well, to be honest with you, I am not sure that I ever did. Maybe it was my old dad describing it to me that made it just as clear as if I'd seen it myself. But it is clear in my mind, and I like to have it there, and now Ol Antoine is gonna do it for me in that old-time way, ent it, Ol Antoine?"

Ol Antoine's mouth watered when he smoked and his cigarette was now sodden at the end and would not draw. He dropped it through a hole in the top of the drum stove, but that was the only reply he made.

"His brains have seized up in the cold," said Smith to Norah. "They will thaw after a while and he will remember some of the English language again."

Smith smoked his cigarette until its red coal ate almost into his thumb and forefinger, which had a deep nicotine tan. Norah gave Ol Antoine some coffee, which he took, and a sharp look to which he did not respond.

"Maybe," said Smith, "I ought to get that Shuswap from down below the Fraser to come in talk to that horse for me. You could give me back the ten dollars I already paid you, and I could bring in that Shuswap. Y'know, Norah, them Shuswaps were really good with horses. They had horses before the Chilcotins got them, didn't they, Ol Antoine?"

"You're wasting your time talking to him on that subject today."

"Also," Smith continued, "I remember that old fellow at Sugar Cane Reserve, he had a great remedy for fixing up frozen ears. An old Intian remety. I don't spose you ever heard about what that Shuswap said to do for frozen ears?"

"He did not come up here to talk about horses or frozen ears," said Norah. "Ol Antoine," she said, loudly, "who is in that cabin with you?"

He looked up at her briefly and then down again into his coffee cup.

"Who is there with you?"

24

"I think you should leave him alone," said Smith.

Norah spoke again, sharply, "Ol Antoine!"

The old man put both hands on his knees and pushed himself up.

"Sit down," said Smith. "We can talk tomorrow about how we get that quarter horse into the corral. Sit down and get warm, Ol Antoine."

The old man walked to the kitchen door. He opened it. A little cloud of steam formed where the warm, moist air of the kitchen mixed with the cold air of the outdoors. Looking back at Smith, Ol Antoine said, "Might be, spose you wear a hat, you don't freeze them ears." Then he left.

"You see," she said, "he wouldn't talk to you because I'm here."

"Oh, I don't think he minds you very much. He is really a very tolerant old man, you know."

"Don't always act the fool, Smith. Don't you know who is in that cabin with him?"

"You mean in the love nest?"

"He has got Gabriel Jimmyboy with him, that's who."

Smith's face became still and a screen seemed to be drawn across his eyes, an annoying habit of his.

"Now why would you say that?" he said.

"Because I know, that is why."

"I see. You know."

"Yes. I know. There is no other man in this country would sneak into that cabin the way

25

that man did. No saddle-horse. Just walked in, a couple of hours after Ol Antoine set himself up in there. Smith, that man has never come out of that soddie in daylight ever since the day you buggered off. Sometimes I catch his shadow near that window, but he never comes out."

"Just for seeing somebody come into that old soddie for a visit, I would say you have worked it all up to a pretty good story."

"It is Gabriel, I tell you. I been scared, Smith. Every morning I went out to feed up I put the baby on the wagon with me. I been afraid even to go out to the wood pile."

"Well, why be scared? I mean, even if it is Gabriel. It ain't Gabriel but, even spose it is, what is there to be all worked up about? He is not bothering you. Why are you all bothered about him?"

"I am bothered because he is a god-dam crazy murderer, that is why."

"There is no harm in Gabriel Jimmyboy."

"No harm? In Gabriel?"

"Well, he has had his disagreements with the law I know . . ."

"The disagreement was murder, and the police have been looking for him since last October."

"November, wasn't it, I think?"

"Well, all right, November. What difference does it make? He has been hiding out from the police all this time and he is a crazy bloody murderer."

26

"Well, in a way, but the only time he ever got in trouble with the law was when he was drunk."

"You mean when he shot Haines."

"Yes. He was drunk as fourteen hundred dollars. Had been for months."

"If he was drunk then he can get drunk again."

"Not on this ranch he can't. I should know. The place has been dry since Cattlemen's Association meeting last October. And Arch MacGregor wouldn't give him any, even sposin he had the nerve to go down there to the store. And there is no whisky to be had in Graveyard Valley."

"Why did you say Graveyard Valley?"

"Oh, I don't know. I had to say something. It sounded more sensible than Calgary or Seattle."

"I think you know where that murderer has been hanging out. He has been up in Graveyard Valley."

"I never said any such thing."

"Dear God," she said, "how I wish somebody could have put a bullet through that damn murderer months ago."

He said, "Norah, I tell you all is well. For one thing, it will not be Gabriel who is down there. For another, even if it should happen to be him, he is a quiet sort of a man. He wouldn't bother you or anybody else."

"It is Gabriel. I know. And you are going to get him out of there."

"Norah, you are all excited."

"Get him out of there. Because if you don't, I am goin to ride down to Arch's store, and get on the telephone, and bring the police in here."

"Now that," he said, "is one thing we do not need on this ranch, is policemen. Quite apart from the fact that you are going to look kind of foolish after they get here, and find it is Macdonald Lasheway or somebody else in the cabin, somebody who is not Gabriel, even apart from that, Norah, I do not feel any need for policemen or any other kind of government people on my ranch."

"Get him off this place," she said, "or I am going to go to Arch's and use the telephone."

"All is well," he said.

"Get him out of here," she said, "or I ride down to get a policeman. Do you hear me . . . ?"

"Oh, all right," he said. "All right, all right, all right all right all right all right. I will go down and tell him to clear out."

He walked to the clothes pegs by the kitchen door and pulled on his coat there, and his overshoes, and as an afterthought he gently fitted a large knitted hat over his small neat head and pulled it down below the points of his ears, remarking, "Spose I wear a hat, might be I don't freeze them ears."

"No, Smith," she said.

"How's that?"

28

"No. I didn't mean for you to go down there now, when it's almost dark."

"Exactly when did you figure I should go there?"

"Well, tomorrow, when Ol Antoine comes back. You can tell him that Gabriel has got to go away from this place."

"I see. Or maybe I should send Gabriel a letter, special delivery, registered, air mail. That would be a lot of help, too, considering that he can't read and there is no mail service here."

"Dammit, all I mean is that I didn't ask you to go down there all alone when it's half dark. Don't go down to that soddie, Smith."

"What is all yellow, weighs six hundred pounds and flies through the air?" he asked, and when she didn't offer an answer gave his own: "Two three-hundred-pound canaries."

He snapped the buckles on the overshoes and opened the door to leave.

"Oh, God," she said, "you're so pig-headed. If you got to go, at least take the gun with you. I'll get the carbine from the sitting-room."

"You leave that gun," he said, "right there where it sits. On the wall. There has been enough of this foolishness without people wavin guns around in the air."

Then he walked out, closing the door firmly behind him, saying, "What has got eighteen slant eyes and catches flies? A Japanese baseball team."

Gabriel

The old cabin was tucked half in and half out of the dry sidehill beside the Oregon Jim Creek. Smith began to sing to himself, loudly, tunelessly, as he neared it. He pounded his feet on the snow, thumped the old grey door loudly before he pushed it open and said very clearly, "Hello, this place. It's me. Smith."

After he shoved the door shut with his heel the only light in that musty old den came from the cracks in the drum stove at the cabin's inner wall. Ol Antoine sat there, speaking rapidly and unusually loudly in Chilcotin. Smith walked over and sat beside him on the bench by the drum stove, ignoring Gabriel, who stood in the corner next the door. The firelight reflected from the hexagon barrel of the old .44-.40 Gabriel held in his two hands, the muzzle pointed at the floor. His eyes were pointed at Smith. They were dark, as were his clothes, his hair and his skin. He was thin and he was quiet. Gabriel was a quiet man. Except for murdering Haines, he had never made much impression upon anybody in thirty or forty years.

Even after a minute or more inside, the old

cabin remained dark as a high-price cocktail lounge. The only window had many of its small panes plugged with rags and cardboard, most of the glass panes being long gone and the weathered wooden frame much too frail to accommodate new ones. The floor was of mud. There was one wide bunk in the room on which was heaped some hay and a few ragged clothes and not much else. Because Gabriel kept very still beside the door, it seemed possible that Smith had failed to notice him or his gun.

Smith began to twist another cigarette and spoke to Ol Antoine, breaking in upon the liquid singsong of Chilcotin with the harsh but clear words of the Chinook jargon.

"Cole illahie," he said. "Hyas cole illahie, Ol Antoine."

Ol Antoine ceased his talk and looked at Smith, who continued to speak, loudly.

"Yeah. I remember what my old dad used to say to me about winters like this. Y'know, he claimed he could remember when he first came to this country: it hit sixty below in March one year. Yes. I remember what he used to say about winters like this. He was a funny old stick, y'know. Dry as a widow's breasts. He used to say . . . Damn!"

The Chanticleer rice paper had torn in his hands and the yellow strands of Vogue tobacco fell in a small heap on the mud floor, between his feet. He looked at them there.

"Funny thing," said Smith softly. "I guess I

31

can't remember what it was my old dad used to say." He laid both hands, palm down, upon his knees and pressed a little. "Ol Antoine," he said, "it's a kind of foolish thing, ent it, your friend takes out a gun when I come in this place? It's only me comes in this cabin. Me. Smith. Don't you spose he's foolish to grab that gun when it's only Smith comes to his cabin?"

"He gets scared this place, Gabriel," said Ol Antoine.

"Well, I don't know who your friend is, but that don't matter. I think that he should lay down that gun and come up here and smoke a cigarette with us."

Gabriel said, "I get scared cause there is only one door this place."

"I know exactly what you mean," said Smith, "but it would be more sensible if you came up and smoked a cigarette and we will talk some. I will twist one for each of us." He started again, blowing a leaf of paper loose at the top of the Chanticleer packet with a light puff of his breath. After he had gently pulled the paper free he turned, for the first time, to look at the corner beside the door. "Come on, friend," he said, "let's light up a smoke."

"You call me friend," said the man in the corner. "What for you don't use my name? My name's Gabriel Jimmyboy."

"Well, then, Gabriel, if you want to be called by name. Gabriel, come up and have a smoke. And kindly put that gun down, will you? It might go off and hurt somebody. Or, the way you got it pointed, blow the last pane out of that window."

Gabriel put down the gun on the floor beside the door and came out of the shadows to sit beside Smith and Ol Antoine. "You know me long time, Smith," he said.

"Well," said Smith, "sometimes I know people quick. Sometimes my memory is awful short. I forget things fast sometimes. Me, I don't know who you are, my friend. You are just somebody stayin in my old soddie cabin a few days with Ol Antoine. I never see your face very good. You see how dark it is here? When you're gone, I don't remember you at all, I guess. Yeah, I don't know anything about you. Not anything." He handed Gabriel a cigarette and a match to light it with.

Ol Antoine said, "Gabriel figures might be you help him so they don't kill him on that rope."

"Oh, I wouldn't know anything about that, Ol Antoine. Your friend is just somebody comes and goes on my place and I never notice. I am a man minds his own business. Always have been that way."

"You're shmart man, Smith," said Gabriel. "Shmart man."

"I can't say that I have noticed it in myself."

"Spose you take me in to them plicemens, Smith, might be we 'range it so they don't kill me on that rope. I'm skert to die that way."

33

"You are going to give yourself up to the police, eh Gabriel?"

"I guess. All them months I'm in that timber, it's hard. It's cole. I figure I go to them plice-mens now."

"Aha."

"You figure that's the best thing for me, Smith?"

"Oh, I guess. . . . Well, I don't know, Gabriel. It is not my business, you understand."

"You think they kill me because I kill that guy Haines?"

"Well, really, I am a poor man to advise you in this kind of thing, Gabriel. Why don't you hunt yourself up a lawyer, first of all?"

"That's what for we see you."

"But I ain't no lawyer. There have been times I thought I ought to learn to read and write and become a lawyer, but I ain't no law-yer. I am a small rancher."

Gabriel found nothing humorous in this remark, which proves, perhaps, the correctness of the old saying that the imminence of death powerfully focuses a man's thinking. He blew thin blue smoke past the red coal at the end of his cigarette. "There's reward for me, ent it?" he said.

"Yes. I believe there is still a five-hundred-dollar reward out for you."

"I guess that gets pretty good lawyer for that much money, ent it? Real smart lawyer."

"Oh, Gabriel, you have got the wrong idea. John Law don't pay you for giving yourself up. He pays that money to the man who brings you in to the police. You understand, it is the man who brings you in. . . ." Smith interrupted himself because of the way that Gabriel was looking at him, looking out of the blue cigarette smoke, out of the darkness beyond the sliver of yellow light from the broken heater, out of quiet eyes, out of the long time when they had not met. "Now," said Smith, "be reasonable, man. How could I possibly manage that?"

"Ain't very hart, I ton't think," said Gabriel softly. "After they give you that reward, all you got to do is give that money to that fella Walter Charlie."

"How did Walter Charlie get into this affair?"

"Walter, he's 'nterpreter that court this year. Knows lots. You give him that money for me, he gets real good lawyer. He tells me that. I know that Walter Charlie long time, and he tells me that."

"You mean I get reward money for you, I give it to Walter and he hires a lawyer with it?"

"Does more than that, I guess. He's 'nterpreter that court. When Ol Antwyne talks for me, Walter Charlie he 'nterprets good for Ol Antwyne," said Gabriel, giving the gentle twang of the Chilcotin dialect to the old man's name.

"What has Ol Antoine got to do with all this?"

35

"He comes that court talks for me. He talks real good and Walter he 'nterprets for that Ol Antwyne."

"Now, Gabriel, Ol Antoine doesn't know anything about any end of that business. Why, he was up in the snow hills with me, chasing moose, the day that Haines was—the day that Haines got killed. He don't know anything about it."

"I think Walter, she fixes up that thing real good, after he gets that money. He 'nterprets real good when Ol Antwyne him in that court."

"Now let me get this straight. Walter gets some of the reward money for himself, because he interprets for Ol Antoine in the trial, in the court, and some of the money Walter gives to the lawyer who defends you?"

"Walter's shmart man. He's same like you, Smith. Shmart."

"I am smart enough that I mind my own business, Gabriel."

"I sure need shmart men, Smith."

"I don't know anything about nothin, Gabriel. You leave me out of all this."

"Ol Antwyne, he's sposed take me in to them plicemens tomorrow. He phones them from that telephone at that store Arch MacKrekor has kot. But he's awful old, that Ol Antwyne. Might be he gets mixed up in the head."

They both looked at the old man, who had apparently retreated to some quiet world of his own where it was always warm and there was

36

plenty of beef every day. "Lots peoples fool old Intian like him," observed Gabriel.

"Nobody is going to do anything to Antoine."

"Yeah, I think might be. He's old man now. Not very shmart in the head any more. I think might be maybe they ton't gif him that money for Walter."

"Well," said Smith, "in my own opinion, I would not want to depend too much on Walter Charlie."

"Then you help me, Smith? Cause you're shmart man, too, same like Walter. You both help me this thing, I think maybe they don't kill me."

"Leave me out of this, Gabriel. I have got nothin to do with it. Like I say, I don't know you are even in this cabin. All I know is Ol Antoine brings some friend here and I never get to see that man's face. Maybe it's Macdonald Lasheway comes with Ol Antoine. Maybe it's Young Alexander. I don't know. When anybody asks me, I don't know."

The conversation went on for a long time, circling in its own first tracks. The second time around Smith remarked that he should kill that old cow he'd brought down today, the one that was bawling outside. On the third circuit he suggested that the best organized of all worlds was one in which Indians helped Indians and whites helped whites and both sides minded their own business. Ol Antoine joined in; his knowledge of English revived as the stove got hotter and redder and the conversation lower and softer. A moon came up. It was still a rather small moon, but the air was clear and the snow of the long home meadow very white so there came to be a quasi-daylight outside and the few panes of the little window were lit by it.

As is common in such conversations, the more vigorously the subject was pursued the more its shape became obscured. Walter Charlie was to get all the reward money. He was to get none of the reward money. The lawyer was to be paid by the Indian Department. The lawyer had been found and had agreed to act. There was no lawyer. What was a lawyer? What did he do? Was he the same as a judge? The police had been phoned yesterday, yes, today, yes, not yet, yes, tomorrow, maybe, next week, yes, last week, yes. Smith drifted along in the soft wash of the Indians' voices, remembering only to refuse to involve himself each time that he was asked. He could count all his heartbeats in his right ear now, where some little gnomes were at work with hatchets and hot irons.

When the fire in the stove burned low and the cold moved in and a log shifted with a sound like *sponk*, Smith stood up, pried open the lid, peered at the red coals and said, "It's pretty late, and I think that fire is pretty well dead. I think it's best we all go to bed now."

"I get some wood real quick," said Gabriel.

"No, let us all go to bed now. Ol Antoine—something I want to say to you in the head. You see this sweater I got? This Cowichan sweater? It's my old sweater. I got a new one now. I leave this old one outside my cabin door tonight. Spose you got some friend needs this sweater, Ol Antoine, you take it tonight. If it's gone, I don't ever notice it. You understand? I don't ever notice it's gone."

"You figure they kill Kapriel with that rope?" the old man said.

"Now, Ol Antwyne, this has got nothing to do with me . . ."

Gabriel, who had gone out for wood, came back through the door with a snap like an elastic band. He reached for the old .44-.40 he'd left on the floor and this time Smith could hear the hammer click back.

"Now, Gabriel," said Smith, "all is well, Gabriel. You are just nervous." As he spoke he walked towards the door, which Gabriel had not closed. The Indian stood pressed into the darkest corner, the gun lined up across the doorway. Smith did not step across the line of the gun's aim but came close enough to the open door to see Norah, standing by a poplar, with the light shining on the .30-.30 carbine he had strictly told her should be left on the wall.

"Why, Gabriel," said Smith, "that is only my wife. You don't have to be ascared of my wife. She has come out to kill that old cow for me. That old cow that has been bawlin all night while we have been talking. That old cow is not gonna make it until spring, so I told my wife she should go out and shoot that old cow tonight and we would butcher her up tomorrow morning. That is what it is all about."

Gabriel did not answer nor move.

Smith stepped in front of the gun's muzzle and past it to the open door. At the door he turned and spoke softly into the dark of the old cabin. "Do not worry, Gabriel. Norah ain't mad at you. All she is mad at is me, as usual." When they did not respond, he continued, "I remember now what it was my old dad used to say to me. You know, I was trying to remember when I come in here tonight? I remember it now. He used to say, 'Every woman has got to have a hobby, and my wife's hobby is gettin mad at me.'" But the cabin was a dark pool of silence, so he added, "Well, it always seemed funny, the way he had of saying it. You pick up that sweater okay tonight, eh Ol Antoine?"

Then he pulled the cabin door firmly shut and walked towards the poplars on the creaking snow. The door's hinges had a droop. The door could not be opened without considerable noise. There would be plenty of time to dodge and run if Gabriel pulled it open. But all was silence behind him and the first sound he heard, except for the whimper of snow beneath his boots, was Norah's voice.

"Are you all right?" she said.

He kept walking towards her. "I do not get mad very often," he said.

"Don't get mad, Smith."

40

"I do not get mad very often, I said—"

"Smith, don't lose your temper."

"—but when I say to leave that bloody gun on the bloody wall that is what I bloody well mean."

He pulled the gun out of her hand and threw it into the snow. It went in with scarcely a sound. The hole it made was a thin blue pencil streak in the light of the moon.

"Well, what did you expect me to do?" she said. "You're down in that cabin with that crazy murderer. I wait and wait up at our place. I can't hear anything. And I know he's got a gun, I know he has."

"So you bring out one of my guns and wave it around at him."

"Well, dammit, I didn't know what to do. I didn't know what to think. I ain't brave like you are, Smith. I don't have nerves like you got."

"You could have some damn sense."

"That's all very well to say, but how do I know what to do? And I'm all alone with the baby in the house."

"My suggestion would be that you look after the baby and I will look after this ranch. Come back into the poplars, that wind is freezing us both."

"Then it is Gabriel Jimmyboy in there, isn't it?"

"I never said that. But even supposing it is Gabriel, he is not harming you or me. I think it is about time we all started minding our own

41

business around this place. Now, go back to the house and make some coffee, will you?"

"You aren't going back into that soddie?"

"No, I am not goin back into the soddie."

"Well, then, why don't you come back with me now?"

"Because I will come back in a minute, that is why."

"And you ain't gonna go back into that place?"

"No, I am not."

"Aren't you scared?"

"No, I am not. Scared of what?"

"Y'know, Smith, sometimes, even after all these years, you can fool me."

"How I wish to God I could. Now will you go back to the house, please?"

She said, "Well, okay," and walked away into the dark of the poplar grove. He watched her go, pulled on his mitts, walked back to where the gun was dropped, fished it out of the snow and went back into the trees and leaned the gun against one of them. He pulled off the right mitt and spread his fingers in a fan. They were all shaking, and so was his hand. He tried to vomit, but only an oily sputum came off his lower lip. "By the Almighty God," he said, "that son of a bitch had that gun pointed right at my guts."

And then, being a man of independent mind, he walked down towards the cabin again, anyway. As he approached he said, "Hey, Antoine.

Don't you forget you got that horse to break for me." He whacked the door, twice, with the bottom side of his mittened fist and added, "I already paid you half, don't forget, and it was going to be done last fall at the very latest." There was no answer, but he was satisfied with this. He put his own gun over his shoulder, holding it near the muzzle, the stock poking up to the sky behind him, and walked back to his own place by the shortest path, and at the damn speed he chose.

When he got inside his house he felt better about almost everything. Norah had crammed both the space heater and the kitchen stove with fresh wood and opened the draughts, and there was a splendid Chinook blowing all through his cabin. He put the gun back on the living-room wall, leaving it loaded, as usual, and drank the bowl of hot cocoa that she had left for him at the side of the stove.

He took the last burning gas lantern in his hand and climbed the ladder-like stairs to the loft where he and Norah and the baby slept. The lantern whispered into his good ear about the delights of long and dreamless sleep under the pleasant weight of heavy patchwork quilts.

It was cold at first, although Norah made a warm spot at his back. He thought she was asleep and was almost there himself when she said, "It was Gabriel in there, wasn't it?"

"Yes, it was Gabriel. But as I said, there is no harm in Gabriel now. And, anyhow, you will be glad to know that he is going in to give himself up to the police."

"He is?"

"Yep. All your worryin was for nothin, as usual. Now let us have some sleep."

It was not as easy to find his way to the beautiful green valley of sleep as he had thought because his ear was now very painful, but he was almost there when she shook his shoulder. "Smith." When he did not respond she shook him again, twice. "Smith."

"Hmhm."

"Smith, wake up."

"What is is it?" now in sudden clarity of voice.

"I been thinking," she said.

"If you can't think in the daytime, why start thinking in the middle of the night?"

"Why is Gabriel giving himself up now, after holding out in the bush so long?"

"Oh, I don't know. He wasn't very clear about that. Although it seems to me there was something about that woman Rosie at Basque Meadows he was living with. She went back in the mountains with him and they had a baby there and the baby died of pneumonia or something, and she pulled out. Anyhow, I suppose with one thing and another he figures it just ain't worth while trying to keep running any more. The winter is too cold for him, just like it's too cold for me."

"I never knew he had a woman with him or

44

that they had a baby. Where would they have buried the baby?"

"Now how would I know that? Under a rock, I suppose. Go to sleep like a good woman, will you." He patted her hip, gently, and then removed his hand and rolled back on his side so that his sore ear was away from the pillow.

"I spose there is no doubt that he killed Haines?"

"No, there is no doubt whatever."

"Well, why did he do it?"

"He did it because he was drunk, and he was drunk because a man we know, whom I need not name, had been keeping Gabriel drunk for the best part of a year."

"I never heard about that. What was it all about?"

"Well, maybe you never heard about it at the time, but there was a sort of a business deal of some kind which involved this here rancher getting some land off of Gabriel. And Gabriel was given unlimited credit at the bootlegger. Think of it. Un*limited* credit. Gabriel stayed drunk almost a year, and one day he happened to have a rifle in his hands when he went to Haines' cabin, and he happened to shoot Haines. Haines was just sort of an accident victim in the whole thing, like a man who gets run down by a truck."

"Maybe in a way Gabriel was, too," she said. "Why didn't any of you whites do anything

45

about this business deal where he got so filled up on liquor?"

"What could we do? His business partner had the money. The bootlegger had the booze and Gabriel had the thirst. There wasn't anything we could do."

"Poor devil," she said.

"Haines, you mean?"

"No, Gabriel."

"Would you mind repeating that, so I am quite sure that I understand you."

"I just said I was sorry for him. Every man's hand has been against him."

"My hand ain't been against him."

"Well, it ain't been *for* him."

Smith sat up in the bed and pushed the clothing down to his knees. He spoke to the far wall. "If I live until they hold the Winter Olympics on the south slope of hell, I will never understand you. In five minutes, in the middle of the night, you have gone from wanting Gabriel Jimmyboy shot to telling me that I ain't doing enough for him."

"All I said was, you could do something. Who is going to help him give himself up to the police?"

"I believe Ol Antoine is taking care of that matter. Him an Walter Charlie have somehow got it all fixed up."

"Walter Charlie! He's as crooked as a dog's hind leg. How far would you trust Walter Charlie, Smith?"

"I would trust Walter Charlie about as far as I can bounce an anvil in a swamp. But that has got nothing to do with it. None of this is any business of yours or mine, Norah." He settled himself beneath the bedclothes again. "One thing I have learned, one of the few things I have learned in my particularly unsuccessful career, is that there is only two times that you get into trouble with Indians. One time is when you try to hurt them and the other is when you try to help them. Me, I just mind my own affairs."

"I suppose you're right." She picked at a piece of bark that clung to the peeled log beside her head. The *snick, snick* of her fingernails kept him awake.

"Do you think they'll hang him?" she said.

"Yes."

"Well, why should they?"

There was no answer.

"Why should they now, when it was so long ago?" She shook his shoulder. "Answer me, Smith."

"If I answer, can I go to sleep then?"

"Yes."

"Well," he said, "the reason is very simple. When Gabriel shot Haines, the first bullet didn't kill Haines. And Gabriel sat in Haines' kitchen, drinking Haines' whisky, while Haines took about two and a half hours to die on the floor in front of him. Gabriel just couldn't be

47

bothered putting the second shot into him. Juries don't like that sort of thing."

"Oh."

After a long pause she said, "Smith, why is everything in this world so hard to understand?"

"It is not hard to understand if you just don't think about it," he said. "Now will you please do me a personal favour and shut up so that we can get some sleep?" Just before he floated to the still water at the bottom of the day's hard current he added, "If you should see my Cowichan sweater hanging outside the back door, don't move it please." She didn't answer him.

He dreamed after all. He didn't plan it like that, but it happened anyway. He was on the quarter horse at the Williams Lake stockyards. He was cutting out heifers. Some men who knew cutting horses well were watching him. Billy Twan, the famous cutting horse man from the Alkali Lake Ranch, was there. Somebody from the Gang Ranch was there, too. Somebody said, "Very nice, very nice," when he got a heifer to the chute. But this was all wrong. It had been slow. The horse wasn't working by itself. He was neck-reining it. He smiled at Billy Twan and pretended he was using the lines as a joke. It wasn't Billy Twan. It was an old, old rancher he should know, an old, old man with a creamy white moustache that fell down on both sides of his mouth. He felt the quarter horse going slacker under him. "You son of a bitch," said the old man, "you bring a horse into my corral in that shape." He smiled because he was embarrassed at not knowing the old man's name. "Dirty, dirty," said somebody else. "Dirty, dirty, dirty." That was why the quarter horse worked so slow. Both his front legs had been broken. The broken ends of the legs flopped out as he dragged himself along. He had to kill the horse but the snow was too deep under the pine and all the meadow was snow, too. He found an old white stick but it broke. He hit it again and again with the small piece of stick. The old cow slavered at the mouth and some of her sputum struck him in the face. The blood was coming out of her, too. He had shot her too high. Every time her heart pumped the blood squirted out all over the snow and the other cattle clustered around it. He was to cut another heifer out but there was too much dust. They were timing him, and he couldn't see in the dust. He drove the irons into the quarter horse and it stumbled and fell down. He would never get him out of this swamp now and it was his old dad's best horse. "I am going to use him for calf-roping really," he kept saying, "he is really a calf-roping horse," but the old man with the blue eyes and yellow moustache wouldn't answer him.

He stayed in bed until almost noon next day. Then he took a gun off the wall and went down in the meadow and shot the old cow that he'd brought in the day before. There wasn't enough meat on it to be worth butchering, so he left her there on the meadow for dog meat. He did, however, take the hide because the hide of an animal perished of starvation makes the best rawhide. Smith was a man well supplied with information of this sort, information for which most of the rest of the world has now little use.

When it was dark again the wind and the temperature were rising and there was a threat of snow in the air. Norah put salve on Smith's ear, which was now the size and colour of a bar of Lifebuoy soap. Then, after washing the supper dishes, carrying out the slop pail, feeding the baby, washing some diapers and doing some sewing, she went to bed early.

Smith stayed up, trying to discover why the radio would not speak to him. He was fiddling around with it, using a hot poker from the firebed of the stove for a soldering iron, when Walter Charlie came in.

Walter Charlie

Walter was lean and tall and long in the face
and head. He smiled a lot. Smith was known to
say that Walter's smile was like the ripple on a
slop pail. Now he looked upon his visitor without any joy whatever and said, as a statement,
not a question, "It's Walter Charlie, ent it."

"Kint of cold tonight, ent it Smith?"

"Cold, and late, Walter."

Walter joined Smith at the kitchen table and
looked toward the coffee pot on the stove.

"Help yourself," said Smith, "I am busy with
this radio." He probed the radio's delicate
interior with a screwdriver and then snapped at
something he found there with a pair of long-
nosed pliers. Walter surveyed this activity with
mild interest as he drank his coffee.

"It's an odd time of night to be visiting,
Walter."

"I see Ol Antoine's been that old cabin you
got."

"Oh? Well, he often shows up and stays that
place a few days."

"You don't see Ol Antoine and his friend at
that place?"

"I'm pretty busy, Walter. I don't find much time for social life."

Smith walked away to the counter, a few feet distant, and began to rummage for parts in an old cigar box.

Walter's voice followed him over there. "I figure might be I find Gabriel Jimmyboy that cabin."

"Oh? That would be an odd idea, it seems to me."

"But Gabriel don't come here?"

"I wouldn't know that, Walter. That wouldn't be any of my business."

"Might be, I think, spose they ride out today, Ol Antoine and Gabriel, they start go that store Arch MacGregor's got."

"Well, Walter, if you knew where they are going, I guess you didn't have to ask me about it in the first place, did you?"

"Some people say, tomorrow policemens come for that Gabriel."

"Oh? That's interesting. Well, Walter, I guess you will want to get some sleep. You can use the old soddie."

"Policemens pay five hundred dollars for Gabriel, some peoples say."

"Well, that, too, I suppose you would know about, Walter. You're going to be interpreter at the court this year I'm told. I imagine you would know about things like that, wouldn't you? Have a good time with your share of the cash, Walter."

Walter Charlie took two steps towards Smith. His voice dropped, but the half-smile was now a three-quarter. "You must be awful shmart man, Smith," he said. "You don't know who comes your cabin. You don't know who is that Gabriel Jimmyboy. You don't know about policemens. You never hear about that reward. And aaaall of a sutten some things you know real good! You're shmart man, Smith."

"All right, Walter. What are you here for? Spit it out of your teeth."

"That's more better, Smith. Let's you and me talk in the head. You got cigarettes?"

"There is rollings on the table. Help yourself."

"I know you know all about this thing, Smith," said Walter. "Ol Antoine, he's this place lots times. He tells you lots, that old man."

"He does not tell me lots, and the last few times he has been around it ain't been social visiting. I have been trying to get him to break a quarter horse for me."

"What's that horse?"

"He's a chestnut, very short-coupled."

"Funny I don't see that horse."

"Well, I don't give a damn whether you saw him or not. He is there."

"Ol Antoine, he seems little bit old for breakin horses. It's more for young cowboy, ent it?"

"Listen, Walter. Get this into your head. I do not give a pinch of cold coonshit whether you believe Ol Antoine can break a horse or whether you believe I got a horse and whether you believe today is Tuesday. My dealings with Ol Antoine right now are concerned with a horse-breaking deal, which amounts to twenty bucks all told, and I have no interest whatever beyond that."

"Twenty dollars ain't much. Maybe you listen for a hundred?"

"No."

"Smith, you don't kid me, Walter Charlie. You know all that deal about Gabriel. Okay. I talk to you real straight. Delate wawa. Straight deal, Smith. Me, I can't take that Gabriel to them policemens. I'm 'nterpreter that court. Spose I get that reward money: it don't look so good."

"Go ahead. If you want to talk, talk."

"Okay then. Ol Antoine, he's witness that case. Ain't good for him, too. Besides he's old, that old man. He forkets. Might be he forkets to take that reward money."

"Well, there will be somebody there to help him remember, I'm sure."

"Smith, best man for that job is you, ent it? Spose we leave now. We ride real quick. We catch up them Ol Antoine and Gabriel. So it's you gives Gabriel to them policemens. There's four hundred dollars for me, one hundred dollars for you."

"You leave me out of this, Walter. I have got nothing to do with it, now or any other time."

54

"It's sure easy hundred dollars, Smith. Hundred dollars goes loooong way this winter." Walter dragged out the word long and then paused, so that they could both consider how very long it was. "It's only right I get four hundred. I 'range it all! It's me tells Gabriel to go to them policemens. It's me talks with that Ol Antoine."

"And who gets the lawyer for Gabriel, and with whose money?"

"That don't matter, Smith. That Indian Department *gives* him lawyer. I know. They give him one free. Anyhow, don't matter much. I guess they hang him anyhow."

Smith rose and picked up his gas lamp. "Walter," he said, "something I have learned in this life is to mind my own business." He started for the bottom of the stairs. "You should try doing that yourself some time, Walter. Be a real experience for you. I recommend it."

"A hundred-fifty?" said Walter.

"Close the door tight behind you, will you?" said Smith, pointing at it.

Samuels

HERMAN SAMUELS
BARRISTER AND SOLICITOR
47 FRONT STREET
WILLIAMS LAKE, B.C.

May 20

DEAR MOTHER,

How is everything in Hamilton? Do hope you
are feeling better.

The enclosed isn't much but thought it might
do as a down payment on Ernestine's course.
You could tell the people that I can sign any
papers that are necessary, taking responsibility
for payments as she goes along. Please send out
any papers required and I will take care of them.
We are all agreed, I know, on the importance of
her education, particularly in view of poor Bill's
sad experiences.

Also, I have taken out a family medical insurance for you all. There is now no reason for any
of you to be hesitant about going to any doctor
you choose, so please understand this. The insurance is already paid for. If you do not use the
doctors now, it will be money wasted. As you

can see by the enclosed papers it takes care of most ordinary illnesses.

Things are going quite well for me. Of course, I would not pretend that they are not a little slow but this was to be expected. Although I did not realize it when I bought this practice, old Mr. Elliott was so old and had been sick for so many years that the practice had pretty well ceased to exist ten years ago. I suppose I should have known this when the price was so low. However, as a result I am really starting from the bottom, in fact starting from nothing, and as you see I am still writing my own letters.

I have been appointed by the court to defend an Indian outlaw named Gabriel Jimmyboy who is accused of murder. Back in Ontario that may sound rather exciting but it seems that there was nothing very colourful about this affair. He just hid out in the mountains for a few months and finally something, hunger I suppose, caused him to let himself be brought in to the police by some other Indian who has, I believe, claimed a reward for doing so. The other Indian is a very old man called Ol Antoine and, rather unfortunately for me, it appears that he is also a defence witness and this may have some effect upon the jury. I must confess that I find the Indians very difficult to talk with. In fact my client will not talk to me at all but I am sure that we will come to an understanding of one another before the trial at the late summer Assizes. Unfortunately he is now far away from me, at Oakalla Prison in Vancouver, and my fee cannot cover visits between Williams Lake and Oakalla.

I met Mr. Edwards from Quesnel in the courthouse here yesterday. I have mentioned him to you before. I thanked him for referring a small debts case to me. It was a bit of trivia too small for him to bother with at this distance, I suppose, but I appreciated it. Then he said, "I hear that we are going to meet at the Assizes this fall, Samuels." "I didn't know you had a case there," I said. "I have all the cases," he said, "I'm taking my turn as Crown Counsel."

I told him that I was certainly relieved to hear that, because I was afraid I was going to be up against somebody really nasty and his manner changed very quickly and he said, "You are, Samuels, you are. That dirty murderer of yours is one that is going to hang, and he should." I tried to explain that I knew he would conscientiously bring out all the evidence but that I was grateful because he was a man who would use only proper means. He smiled a hard smile at me and said, "Proper, and if necessary improper, Samuels," and then he walked away. I don't suppose he meant that, really, but I confess I find this hard to take. It is not just that he is an old well-established and respected lawyer of this district with a huge practice, while I am just a little clerk in a ragged gown. I know that everybody has to start out some time at the bottom.

The sad truth is, Mother, that even when I am Mr. Edwards' age I will not be so suave or so wise. He is brilliant and I am not, and neither time nor any sort of success can ever alter that.

Well, I am sounding much too pessimistic but I am concerned partly because it is my first murder case. Do not forget to send me papers to sign for Ernestine's course.

Your loving son,
HERMAN

HAMILTON
May 28

DEAR HERMAN,

Thank you very much for your help, which is appreciated as you know. Unfortunately the money for Ernestine's course is not needed and am sending it back to you in this letter. Ernestine has married a chap almost as young as she is. He has some kind of job at the mill. The whole thing something I would rather not discuss.

Have had very warm spring here and many flowers. Both younger boys still managing to keep up school grades to passing; am hoping they will continue, although pressures to leave always strong.

Your Father is as usual.

Did not like your remarks about other lawyer, more brilliant than me, etc. This very close to self-pity, than which nothing worse. Of course you are not brilliant nor ever will be. Not your birthright. This has nothing to do with your work.

Excuse cramped handwriting.

Affectionately,
MOTHER

HERMAN SAMUELS
BARRISTER AND SOLICITOR
47 FRONT STREET
WILLIAMS LAKE, B.C.

May 1

DEAR MR. SMITH,

I must apologize for having failed to obtain your initials but am addressing this care of Half Diamond S Backwards Ranch, which I am assured will ensure your receiving it.

My request is an unusual one and I am only sorry that distance prevents my driving out to your ranch to discuss this with you. I have been appointed counsel for Mr. Gabriel Jimmyboy who is accused of murder and, being indigent, has been provided with legal counsel by the Federal Government. My client, as I believe is well known, is accused of murdering a James Haines some months ago. I realize that you have no personal knowledge whatever of that particular matter but possibly you have some evidence which could be helpful to the court and jury in reaching a decision in this affair.

The general character of Mr. Jimmyboy may well be a factor in reaching such decisions. Since

I understand your ranch is one of those not far from the Namko Indian Reserve, could it be that you are acquainted with Gabriel Jimmyboy and would you be in a position to come to court to testify that in your experiences with him he proved to be a person of good character?

Please let me emphasize that you would not become involved in any questions as to how Mr. Haines came to his death or by whose hands. You would be asked only to state that you knew Gabriel Jimmyboy to be a person of good character—if, as I trust, that is the case,

I would very much appreciate an early answer.

Yours truly,
HERMAN SAMUELS

∧ ⌒ RANCH
NAMKO, B.C.
June 14

DEAR MR. HERMAN SAMUELS,

My husband has been very busy with spring roundup, branding, etc., for the past month or so and has not had much time to answer your letter so he asked me to do so. He says he does not have any evidence that would be of any use to you because at the time of Haines murder he was up in the mountains hunting moose. Hoping this will oblige.

Yours sincerely,
NORAH SMITH

61

NATIONAL BANK OF MONTREAL
WILLIAMS LAKE BRANCH

June 1

P. E. I. Smith, Esq.,
Half Diamond S Backwards Ranch
Namko, B.C.

DEAR MR. SMITH,

My name will not be known to you. I have
recently taken over managership of our Williams
Lake branch from Mr. Williams, who has been
transferred to Edmonton.

I regret that our association must begin in
these terms. However, your account is in very
serious disarray and I am sure you will understand why it has been necessary for me to put a
stop to all cheques drawn upon this account.

It will be necessary for you to come immediately to Williams Lake to discuss new arrangements for settlement of your account. I cannot
stress too strongly the seriousness and urgency of
this matter.

Yours truly,
JOHN L. HAAKON

V ∽ RANCH

NAMKO, B.C.

July 20

DEAR MR. HOKON,

You are not any more worried about that
account than I am and something has got to be
arranged right away.

62

I will be in with the beef drive in a couple of months and you will be the first man I look up when I hit town.

Yrs truly,
SMITH

HERMAN SAMUELS
BARRISTER AND SOLICITOR
47 FRONT STREET
WILLIAMS LAKE, B.C.

July 8

John Hamilton, Esq., Barrister and Solicitor
Harvey, Hamilton, Harvey and Jones
500 Granville
Vancouver

PERSONAL

DEAR JOHN,

Have been watching your career through the newspapers. Soon I will be able to say, "I knew him when." My sincerest congratulations: we all knew yours was what can truly be called the legal mind.

Recalling that you offered me a hand last fall while you were passing through town on your hunting trip, I would like to take advantage of it.

I've been appointed to defend an Indian named Gabriel Jimmyboy on a murder charge. You may not have heard of the case. His arrest got very little space in the metropolitan press, in fact it did not even gain much prominence in the local weekly. It is one of those rather sordid murders and, having occurred almost a year ago, all details are vague except the police technical evidence which, as it emerged at the preliminary, seems solid as Mount Robson. Not only do they have the gun, ample fingerprints and motive of robbery, they have also strong medical evidence that the victim died very slowly, over a period of about two hours, and that the murderer was in cabin with him during that time and offered no first aid but rather ignored the dying man. You can imagine the effect of this upon a jury.

I feel quite sure that liquor played a part in this but can find no witnesses who know anything about anything whatsoever. My client is, to put it in the mildest of terms, unco-operative. He has arranged for an Indian called Ol Antoine to attend the Assizes to give evidence, incidentally the same man who collected a $500 reward for bringing my client in to the police, but beyond assuring me at a brief and unsatisfactory meeting that he would be present (and this through an interpretation of my client's) the old man has not enlightened me in any way and he is now hundreds of miles distant from me and unavailable.

Under the circumstances it is hardly likely that you or anybody else can succeed in gaining Jimmyboy's confidence, since I exerted myself so very strenuously and, I thought, tactfully, and failed utterly. However, I am responsible for doing the best that I can and my conscience would bother me if I didn't make every effort, including enlisting help from an old schoolmate.

Your burgeoning criminal practice takes you often to Oakalla. Could you just take a few minutes to see Jimmyboy (I'll enclose a note to the warden) and point out to him that if he was drunk at the time of the murder it would be very important to point this out to the jury and that I might bring witnesses from the Namko Reserve to testify to this? We might not want to use such evidence, but we should consider it. He speaks English and will understand you, no matter how unresponsive he may seem.

I fear it's hopeless, but would appreciate you giving a few minutes of your time, John.

Very best regards,
HERMAN SAMUELS

JOHN HAMILTON
BARRISTER AND SOLICITOR
HARVEY, HAMILTON, HARVEY AND JONES
500 GRANVILLE
VANCOUVER

July 14

Herman Samuels, Esq.
Barrister and Solicitor
Williams Lake   PERSONAL

DEAR HERMAN,

Thank you for your letter of recent date.
You are a hard-luck man in picking cases, old

boy. Who was the unkind friend at Williams Lake who appointed you to defend this one?

I visited your obsidian-eyed friend who wears his hair helmet-style. He has a bad case of adenoids, I believe, and hisses through missing teeth when he breathes. The result was negative, *nada*, nothing, nothing, nothing. When I got to him it turned out he didn't know any English whatever. I have had more reaction in talking to the stone lions at the front of the Georgia Street Courthouse.

Judging by the lack of sunniness in his personality and your description of the messiness of the murder, I would think he's a poor insurance risk at the moment. Perhaps you're better off without witneses. Remember what the dean used to say—the only unbreakable case is the one in which no evidence is brought forward to be challenged.

Recalling that abundant conscientiousness of yours, you will probably put far more time and energy in this case than the fee or any normal interpretation of the word duty could demand, but I say to you in all seriousness, fall back on the old slogan, "Collect your fee in advance, and console yourself with the thought that you don't have to serve the sentence."

All the best to you, Herman. Don't forget to give us a ring when you're in the city.

Yours truly,
JOHN HAMILTON

Frenchie Bernard

❦

Over the months as spring's mud hardened, as the new grass came briefly green and then quickly toasted to its usual ground-cure of brown, as the cattle went back to the high summer range and the two older boys came back from school and were set to work building yet more miles of Russel and Buck fencing, the quarter horse continued to enjoy the good life.

Smith had intended to hold him on the Jimmie Meadow, which was not far from the Home Place, but the quarter horse found or made a hole in the fence. He went back into the high hills, taking a harem of mares with him. He picked up a pair of mares from Frenchie Bernard as he went.

Frenchie complained of this elopement to Smith. Smith was surprised at his attitude. His quarter horse, he said, was merely improving the Bernard horse herd.

No harm could come from better breeding, he said. And then, in a reference to Frenchie's squat build, Smith remarked that it would be a better thing for the country if he, Smith, had married Frenchie's wife; she could have had children whose ass would have been a little further off the ground. Frenchie was not amused.

Smith and Frenchie spent two days hunting the stud and his mares and colts and bringing them back.

During these two days Smith had ample time to discuss what he conceived to be the old Indian way of breaking horses by talking to them, but he could not arouse much interest. Frenchie said only, "What is a quarter horse, anyhow, except a thoroughbred with some brains put in it?"

Their parting was cool, considering the fact that they were next-door neighbours, living only five miles apart.

And Ol Antoine Again

There are only two seasons of the year in Namko, winter and August. August is sometimes very hot. It was an afternoon late in that month, a day that was one long boil of searing heat, that Ol Antoine came to break the quarter horse.

Smith did not see him for some time, for the old man stood his horse quietly under the blueblack shade of the pine trees at the edge of the flaming yellow pool of grass on the meadow.

The yellow grass was only about a foot high and, if the truth be known, not particularly nutritious. The Ripgut grass was all right, but this was just swamp hay. It lay under water much of the year. It had never been ploughed or even harrowed. It had been improved only by ditching at its upper edge, a process of many years of hard labour. In turning water away to the creek bed by ditches, Smith had succeeded in drying the meadow somewhat and the type and quality of the grass had improved slightly as a result. He had five hay meadows such as this.

Norah had many times insisted that he get literature from the Department of Agriculture to see how they might improve their grass crops, but he usually forgot or failed to answer her. Once he had remarked, "Hell, I'm not running this place half as good as I know how to already."

Now he was on the seat of his old horse-drawn mower, which went clattering, clanking, jingling over the bumpy floor of the meadow, beaten rock-hard by the brazen hammer of the sun. The mower blade was high. It had to be to clear the uneven ground, and the stubble it left seemed almost as high as the grass it scissored down. But every little bit helped because the hay had run out in the previous winter, as Norah had predicted, and nine of the breeding stock had died, as she had anticipated.

The big meadow was dotted with colour and astir with action.

The two horses that drew the mowing machine were big bays. The machine was black except for its shiny white chattering teeth. Smith's shirt, which he wore buttoned down to the wrists and almost up to the neck, was blue and so were his Levis. He wore a red nylon kerchief around his neck. The Indian women, among Macdonald Lasheway's hay crew a mile up the meadow, wore billowing cotton print dresses of many colours. The gin pole with which they stacked the hay had acquired the soft and lovely grey of old age. At the meadow's foot, hidden from Smith by a roll of the grassland, Sherwood and Roosevelt were raking hay and their horses, too, were of many colours, chestnut and brown and one gaily splashed Paint who seemed to have stepped out of the frame of one of Remington's paintings. The islands of poplar showed white and a delicate green; west, beyond the pines, was the cool white crust of mountains that never lost their snow.

Yet there was a hard, bleached, almost bitter quality to the scene and colour could not relieve it. Everything was dominated by the brassy light from the sun. It hurt the eyes and cooked the skull and made the creek run slower. Even the stir of action was diminished by it. Flickering columns of heat haze stood between Smith and the stacking crew, making the figures of the Indians flicker and shift as they went about their work. The songs of the birds were listless and few.

Ol Antoine did not stir his horse while the mower battered its way up the grass towards him. Smith was within twenty yards of the old man before he noticed him. He did not turn his head or give any indication that he had seen the rider. Instead he drove the mower abreast of the point where Ol Antoine stood before he reined in. Then he slowly turned to look. He used one of the few words of the intricate Chilcotin language known to him.

"Koneesta'ah, Ol Antwyne."

"Konista'ah."

Ol Antoine walked his cayuse out of the shadow of the tree and stopped him beside the mower. He remained in the saddle and Smith remained upon the seat of the mower.

71

"Waum illahie," said the old man, and Smith agreed that it was hiyu waum.

"I come break that quarter horse you kot," said Ol Antoine.

"Is that right? Why, y'know, Ol Antoine, somebody told me you was dead. But I guess they must have been wrong."

"Don't take me very long, I break that horse now."

"Well, go to it, by all means. He is over on the Jimmie Meadow. I imagine you can catch him."

"Might be you pay me now?"

"Ol Antoine, I have already paid you ten. Now you have got ten more coming when the job is done. When the job is done I give you the other ten." He lifted his black hat and wiped his wet hair. The sweat came down his forehead and cheeks and made lines in the dust. "Half in advance, half when you're done."

"Sure too bad you can't pay me that money now."

"Why do you need it now? You are going to break the horse now. As soon as you're done I give you the money."

"I break that horse right now after I go that court for Gabriel."

"You do it *when*? You mean you are going to Williams Lake, and I am to pay you ten more dollars for not doing that work for me?"

"It ain't you pays me. It's me pays you."

Smith considered this interesting statement in silence for a moment. Then Ol Antoine continued.

"I give you back that ten tollars for kes for him truck. When you drive Williams Lake with me I pay for all them kes."

"If I understand the way this conversation is going, and I am beginning to think I do understand it, you mean I stop haying, I forget about the horse and I drive you two hundred miles to Williams Lake?"

"Sure good, spose you come that courthouse with me. Right away we come back I break that horse you kot."

"You mean I also go into the court with you?"

"You're shmart man, Smith."

"I am a hell of a lot smarter than you think I am. Now listen, I am going to talk slow to you in the head, and you listen, okay? I am not going to get mixed up in this trial. And I am not going to drive to the Lake with you. And if you are smart you will not go there yourself. You understand? Don't you go to that court."

"I go there talk for that fella Kapriel."

"Listen, you don't know anything about that Haines business. You have got nothing to say that anybody in that court wants to hear. And if you make some cultus wawa in there you are going to be in trouble. You understand me? You know what I'm saying? You are goin to be in trouble."

"Only couple days I got to be that place."

"Ol Antoine, I tell you what I will do, although God knows why. I tell you what I will do. You stay here, you do that job for me,

73

startin right today. Not tomorrow. Not pretty
soon some time. Not just right away. You start
today. You break that horse. I pay you thirty
dollars. Thirty dollars instead of twenty dollars.
Ten you got already. Twenty more when that
quarter horse is broke."

"Sure nice. Thirty tollars." Ol Antoine smiled.
He was a simple man and liked simple things,
such as money. He then used a word not common to his speech. "Thanks," he said.

"Okay then, you start today."

"Might be you give me ten tollars now?"

"What for, dammit?"

"There's ten tollars you give me loong time
ago . . ."

"Yes, one hell of a long time ago."

". . . and you give me ten tollars now . . ."

"Go on."

". . . after I talk for Kapriel, I come back. I
break that horse. You give me that other ten
tollars. That's thirty tollars, ent it?"

Smith took off his hat and peered inside it,
but there was no help there. "Ol Antoine, as I
see it there is only one hope left for you. We
are going to have to put you in the government
and they can make you a minister of finance."

The old man began to talk to himself, or to
someone his fancy provided, in the Chilcotin
tongue.

Smith got off the mower, walked over and
placed his hand on the saddle-horse's withers,
almost touching Ol Antoine's bony thigh.

74

"Just try to understand this," he said. "Spose you go to that court, you get in trouble, and I pay you only twenty dollars to break that horse. Spose you stay this place, you got no trouble, I pay you thirty dollars."

"I talk for Kapriel."

"You do not have to talk for Gabriel, and don't let anybody tell you that you do."

"He's my own peoples."

"Well, by God he is not my own peoples and I am not paying you any money in advance and I am not driving you to the Lake and I am by God sick and tired of talking about it, too."

He got back on the mower, shook the lines and said, "Haaahh! You shitters."

Ol Antoine watched him go. The back of Smith's grey shirt was now marked with sweat in two long oval patches. It was too bad that white men smelled so bad when they sweated. Like rancid butter. Ol Antoine, who had far too little body fluid left to spare any more sweat in his life, walked the horse back under the shade of the trees. His head tipped forward, he was thinking again. He was concerned. The trial, he knew, must start soon.

How soon was not entirely clear. Although the trial was one of the main topics of conversation on the Reserve, the time of it kept shifting, each person offering his own estimate.

Ol Antoine felt that for a trial, as for the annual stampede that was the Namko's great social event, the best way of arriving on time was to go days earlier than the earliest estimate of the date. People from the remoter Reserves who didn't do this for the stampede, he had noted, often didn't arrive until the second or third day and thereby missed much of the robust entertainment. Now, he felt, was the time that he must leave for the trial, not two days hence when most of the band planned to go.

He sought out Narcisse Peter at the Reserve. Narcisse had recently spent a summer's hard work with a slashing gang and had spent the abundant wages collected upon a huge old Packard, which now stood at the Reserve's edge with the liver out of it. Narcisse tried to explain to Ol Antoine why the car would not go even if the tires were filled with air, but the Chilcotin language or the old man's knowledge of mechanics seemed inadequate. Finally Narcisse burst out in English, "I tell you I throw him in backup for stop, she's all spoil."

Ol Antoine grunted and went away to see his nephew, Cyrus.

Cyrus James was a prominent womanizer of the Namko Reserve. He was at this time in the concluding phases of a campaign to win Mrs. Jonah Silloo, whose current spouse was not Mr. Jonah Silloo. If Cyrus's wooing should be successful, as he confidently expected, it was his intention to miss the trial of Gabriel Jimmyboy entirely. Instead he would go to a nearby lake and there he would net trout, which Mrs. Jonah

Silloo would gut, bone, slice, spread in the sun to dry and later stack. At evening they would watch the interesting patterns made by mud hens upon the scarlet lake waters and listen to the talk of these birds. The dark of the nights would be filled with soft murmurings and gentle laughter and love.

Cyrus James did not want to take Ol Antoine to Williams Lake.

However, Ol Antoine made his request loudly, unmistakably and in the presence of witnesses. He was a relative of Cyrus, and also he was a very old man. Cyrus found it necessary to agree to go.

They rode to the Lake on the back of a freight truck that was generally known as The Stage.

The departure of Ol Antoine and Cyrus appeared to give the Reserve the vital spark with which to start its engine. Suddenly the movement to the Lake was general. Rides were arranged with ranchers who were taking their trucks there for other, less vital purposes. One old truck on the Reserve was revived sufficiently to pack two whole families towards the east.

Near the Fraser the little migration merged with a few other Chilcotins who, being closer to the town, were making their way there in wagons. At the Lake they would set up their tents on the stampede grounds and there all would hold long conversations in the evenings, when the courts were no longer open. About twelve families attended the trial of Gabriel Jimmyboy.

77

Late in the afternoon of Ol Antoine's conversation with Cyrus, the migratory instinct awakened in Macdonald Lasheway, Smith's hay contractor. All stacking ceased. The horses were harnessed to his wagon. His wife, children, relatives and other members of the hay-contract crew perched upon it and Lasheway brought them all down through the meadow, headed for the Reserve and thence to the Lake.

In the cooling air of the sunset Smith had enjoyed a new vigour. He had harnessed fresh horses to his mower and was circling the ever-narrowing island of his cut at a good speed. He was even singing to himself. When Lasheway's wagon came past he halted the mower team and looked at Lasheway as though anxious to memorize his face.

"You seem to be on the way somewhere," he said.

"Yeah. Little time, I guess."

"What about the hay contract, Macdonald?"

"We get that hay in sure, Smith. Not very long I don't think we're gone. We go see that trial they got for Gabriel."

"Yeah, and spose that weather breaks, maybe I lose almost all my hay again this year. How about that Macdonald?"

Macdonald looked at the sunset, which was an undistinguished one.

"I think he shtays hot," he said.

"You contracted the job, didn't you?"

"Sure. We come back real quick. She shtays reaaal hot this year, I think."

Smith went back to the mower and kept cutting.

Then he rode down the meadow and told the boys not to quit for supper. They could eat after, when it was too dark to work.

When the moon was hanging above the mountain like a Chinese paper lantern, the three of them went home on their saddle-horses.

"Why so late?" said Norah, "This is only the start of haying. We got lots of time this year."

"Maybe," he said.

"The hay crews pulled out," said Sherwood. He was thirteen and, being almost of man's estate, sometimes joined in such conversations.

"The hay crews *what*?"

"Smith talked to them, but they went anyhow," said Roosevelt.

"You let the hay contractors pull out?"

"Well, it wasn't exactly a matter in which they were interested in my advice. They seemed to have made up their minds already."

"When will they be back?"

"Who can tell?" he said. "With luck, they will come back after all the singing and dancing at the Assizes is over, which would be in about a week. Otherwise they may wait until the rain or the snow make it unnecessary for us Smiths to make hay any more."

"And you let them go?"

79

"As I say, I didn't have much choice. I suppose I could of got mad and jumped through my hat, but somehow I don't think it would have made a very deep impression on them."

"You idiot! This is the one time you should have got mad."

"Now, Norah, all is well."

"Oh, go to hell," she said. "And you can dish up your own supper, too." She started up the steep stairs to where young John was beginning to mutter about the milk shortage. As she went, she spoke to herself: "Our first good spell of weather in three years to get a hay crop. My God!"

Smith dished up stew for himself and the boys. "Your mother has a very even temper," he said, "she is mad all the time."

Exeter, aged nine, joined the conversation. He was a solemn child with a distinctive personality. One of his gifts was that of mimicry. When he imitated somebody, he could make even the grammar fit. His parents and brothers were never certain whether Exeter was conscious of his ability as a mimic and proud of it or if he was, perhaps, a sort of witless freak like a circus horse. Now he imitated Norah, without revealing whether or not he knew he was doing so.

"There is only enough in the bank for the hay contractors," he said, "that is all. That is what we have got to realize."

The tone of voice and the current of the words were not his. They were Norah's, Norah seated at the old escritoire in the living-room, making up the accounts, her glasses resting half way down her short nose.

"We have got to realize that if we don't get hay this year we are broke."

"Well, Exeter," said Smith, "we have taken care of that by having the hay crews pull out. This way we may not get enough hay but, on the other hand, we will not have to pay the hay crews, so we will save money in that way. Maybe there will even be some beer money left over in that account."

Exeter did not step out of character. "I hope so, Smith," he said, in Norah's voice, "because if we go into the hole another year there is nothin left but to sell out. That is the only thing. That is what we will have to do. Sell out."

"Besides," said Exeter, "everything is so dry right now it wouldn't surprise me if we got a fire across the meadows. That would be just our luck."

"I have taken precautions about that," said Smith. "Do you notice I have stopped smoking and am using chewing tobacco again?"

Exeter speared a piece of meat and chewed it slowly and swallowed. This time he answered in his own voice. "I guess that's a good thing," he said.

Young Alexander

Four days later it was just as hot. In the night they opened all the doors and windows to catch the cool draught that came slowly down the slopes from the mountains after dark. About nine each morning Norah closed the doors and windows, drew the curtains and hung blankets over those windows that faced the sun. In this way the log house retained its coolness longer, although by the time the day's heat had peaked, about four P.M., the cabin temperature had climbed to meet it.

It was about that burning hour of the day when Smith came home, unexpectedly, and stepped into the darkened house. Norah was using the treadle sewing machine beside a sliver of light that came though the kitchen window. She felt relaxed. Sewing machines did that for her. They had a precision that she had failed to find in a husband. "Hi," she said, "you're back early."

"Rawtheh wahm for tennis today, Chauncey, daon't you think?" he said. He pulled off his shirt. The sun had burned his hands, his face and a short V beneath his neck almost black. In

82

contrast the rest of his torso was startlingly white. His ribs were showing. He was, Norah noticed once again, rather pigeon-chested.

He lifted a dipper of water from the galvanized pail that stood beside the kitchen door on a small board bench. He raised the water to his lips but did not drink. Instead he lifted the dipper high and slowly poured the water over his head. It streamed down his front and back and splashed on his pants and on the floor.

"If I owned both hell and this place," he said, "I think in summer I would rent out this place and live in hell."

He took another half-dipper of water. From his pocket he took his Epsom salts bottle and dropped a fraction, about a quarter-teaspoon, into that water. He replaced the cap on the bottle, put it back in his pocket, brought the dipper to the table and sat there, sipping very lightly.

"Did something break again?" she said.

"Yep. Mower blade."

"Can you fix it again?"

"I think it will take another weld, although really I would be smart to have a spare on hand. I should get one sent in from the Lake on the stage."

"Well, you know we can't write any cheques for it."

"It's only about fifty bucks' worth of parts I need for that mower right now; however, I could

83

charge them. My jawbone is good with Clanceys, I guess."

"No. If we have got to do that, let's go into the link money."

In the long previous winter Rappaport had trailed and treed four lynx, which Smith had shot, skinned and sold. Border collies such as Rappaport were not supposed to understand the trail-hound business, but he was an unusual dog.

"Good old Rap'ort," said Smith, "Eighty bucks, wasn't it?"

"Yes."

"Well, okay, we will spend that. I don't spose there is any news about the trial?"

"The radio hasn't worked for a month, Smith."

"No, that's right, it hasn't. One thing I can't weld up. Maybe we should send it into town, too."

"It would sure be nice to know something about what's going on in the world."

He was drinking more deeply from the dipper now, as his body had cooled, and he was enjoying the tang of the water. "Speaking of world affairs," he said, "I wonder if Ol Antoine is finally goin to break that horse for me this year, when he comes back?"

"Oh, you and that damn horse!"

"I am a man of very simple ambition. Some men want to be prime minister. Some men want to play the piano in the cathouse. But what I want is to have Ol Antoine do that horse job for me." He thought about it some more. "Yep," he said, "Norah, when the hay is all in this fall, and before fall round-up starts, you know what I am goin to do?"

She did not answer, but he didn't expect her to so it made no difference.

"That last load of hay is not going to go on any stack. It is coming right back here, to the yard of this house. I am going to dump it there. It is goin to be twenty-seven feet from the kitchen door, and twenty feet up from the creek, and fifteen feet from the snubbing post. Every morning, at nine o'clock exactly, I am going to go out and I am going to lay me down on that pile of hay." His eyes were fixed far away and his voice became very soft. "In my right hand, not my left hand, not the left you understand, but in my right hand I am going to hold a full bottle of whisky, THE CAP OF WHICH HAS BEEN THROWN AWAY. I am going to lay me there in that hay, and I am going to sip that whisky, and I am going to watch Ol Antoine talk to that quarter horse. It may be that some of the time Ol Antoine will not be there. Maybe, in fact, even the horse will not be there. But I will be there. I will see them, just the same. And I will be the happiest small rancher in all the Cariboo country."

"You're using Epsom salts too much to beat this heat," she said. "I'll make you a sealer of lime juice."

"I intend to start this job at nine o'clock

85

every morning and to wind it up with a nap at about three in the afternoon. It will be, I think, a five-day job. Using a separate bottle of whisky for each day, of course."

Young Alexander arrived just in time to share in a drink of lime juice, a pale and astringent brew served without sugar in mugs that had once contained peanut butter.

Young Alexander was an old man, although not of the stage of near-mummification reached by Ol Antoine. He was a power of sorts on the Namko Reserve and owned two cows and six horses. Who the Old Alexander was, from whom Young Alexander had been differentiated, had long since been forgotten by almost everybody.

He seemed perturbed.

"What's the matter, Young Alexander?" said Smith. "You seem all excited."

"I got something I got to tell you real quick."

"Well, as long as it isn't anything serious you can go ahead. Just don't tell me that the government has changed, that's all. I have got to depend on the present government to keep the sun shining this way into October. No other government could do that. I'm sure of that."

"It's 'mportant. It's Ol Antwyne tells me talk to you."

"Aha. News from Ol Antoine, eh?"

"He's in chail, that old man."

"In jail, you say! Well, I am not surprised, Young Alexander. That is what I told him would happen. I warned him and I warned him until I was tired of talking to him. I told him to stay away from that murder trial."

"He kets all mixed up apout that."

"I knew he would get all mixed up. That's what I told him. I said stay away from that Jimmyboy trial. I suppose that Walter Charlie was his usual self in this business?"

"Walter Charlie ain't in that court."

"He ain't there, eh? Where was he?"

"It ain't that court Ol Antoine goes. He gets all mixed up. He goes in that small court."

"You mean he went into the magistrate's court instead of to the Assizes?"

"I kess."

"Well, what happened?"

"Somebody in that small court, he calls for an Intian named Abraham. Ol Antoine, he don't hear so good; he says, 'Yes.' That chutch in that small court, he says, 'Abraham, these policemens says you get trunk last night.' Ol Antoine, sometimes he forkets all how to talk in English. He just says, 'Yes.' That chutch puts him in chail for five days."

"Well," said Smith, "there is new ways to get into trouble in this world after all. I thought they had all been discovered, some of them by me, but Ol Antoine has found a brand-new way to get into trouble. He goes to the wrong court, answers to the wrong name and goes to jail on the wrong charge. Yes, there is no doubt about it. He has set some kind of a record."

87

"Ol Antoine says might be you come get him out of that chail."

"Well, Young Alexander, don't fret about that. It might be a good thing if he just stays in there for a few days until that trial of Gabriel's is over. He's safer in there, really."

"He says he kot to ket out of that place."

Norah said, "He shouldn't be in jail, Smith."

"No, he shouldn't, of course. But then, if he wants out it is easily done. Young Alexander, it is very easy for Ol Antoine to get out of that jail. All he has to do is tell them who he really is. They will check up and when they find out who he is they will let him out."

"He won't do that thing."

"Why won't he do that thing? That is, apart from the usual reason of being so stubborn."

"He's 'shamed, that old man. He ain't ever been in him chail before. He's 'shamed."

"Well, I spose being in jail is a thing you've got to get used to, like everything else in this life," said Smith.

"Poor old man," said Norah.

Young Alexander said, "Spose he gives that chutch ten tollars, that chutch he lets him ko."

"That is what is called a fine," said Smith. "He don't really pay the judge. He pays a fine. The reason he is in jail is that he didn't pay the fine. I would imagine that this sentence was a ten-dollar fine or five days imprisonment. Yeah, that's what it would be. Ten dollars or five days."

Young Alexander stirred restlessly and in

88

some irritability. All whites talked too much, but Smith was one of those who could usually curb that instinct at appropriate times. Now he, too, was howling, as dogs do at a moon. Young Alexander spoke with some vehemence. "That's what I said, ent it? That judge lets him go if Ol Antoine gives that judge ten tollars."

"Well, then, surely Ol Antoine can pay ten dollars. He got to Williams Lake, so he has found transport and money some place. He can find ten dollars to pay the fine of whoever it is whose sentence he has got to serve." Smith sucked in some lime juice and spoke again. "There is a limit to my interest in this business, Young Alexander. I have lost my hay crews on account of this trial of Gabriel Jimmyboy. I am runnin the risk of losin my hay crop. The banker is lookin at me with his glass eye. My wife's pregnant again."

"I AM NOT."

"Well, now, you see, there is always some good news among the bad, if you will just look for it. She is not. But generally, Young Alexander, the Smith news is not good."

Young Alexander smacked his glass down upon the old cracked linoleum of the table. "What's all this funny talk?" he said. "Son a bitch, you pay Ol Antoine that money you owe him, he gets out of that chail."

"What money is that, exactly?"

"He breaks that quarter horse for you, you're sposed pay him thirty tollars."

89

"Oh, yes," said Smith.

"Thirty?" said Norah. "It was twenty, wasn't it, Smith?"

He winced. "Thirty," he said, low-voiced.

Young Alexander did not heed this exchange but continued louder, angrier. "All peoples *know* Ol Antoine he breaks that quarter horse you kot. What for you don't pay him?"

"I already paid him ten," said Smith.

"What for you don't pay him *all* that money? He breaks that horse for you and you don't pay him?"

"All I can say is that it would be awful long and hard to explain," said Smith.

"Damn poor shit, I think," said Alexander.

Smith saw his wife laughing. He stood up.

"I tell you what I will do, Alexander. I will scratch out a twenty-dollar bill here for Ol Antoine, and you can ship it out to him, so he can pay his fine and get out of jail. Mind you, it will prevent me from paying cash on my new mower blade prob'ly, but I realize that is no concern of yours. I will give you that twenty dollars I owe Ol Antoine for breaking that horse for me, and you send it to him and he will get out of jail."

"Okay," said Young Alexander, adding, "I don't know why you don't pay him long time ago."

"I don't know myself, Young Alexander. I guess I am getting old or something. It just went completely out of my head, that Ol Antoine had broke that quarter horse for me. Yep, that is the trouble. I get old and I forket things in the het now, Aleksanter."

"Sure too bad, you don't come that place get Ol Antoine out of that chail your own self."

"No. Now that I will not do. I will give you the money. But I will not go to that court. In fact, I will not go to that place while that trial he is on. I am goin to mind my own business on my own ranch, Alexander. Norah, would you get twenty bucks for our friends, please."

She went to rummage in the back of the kitchen cupboard while Smith and the Indian stood.

"Sure too bad, you don't help that old man," said Alexander. There being no answer, he continued, "He likes you, that old man."

"I think I will have a rollings again. There is no danger of setting fire to a meadow inside this cabin, I don't think. You want a smoke, Alexander."

"He likes you lots."

"Aha," said Smith, pulling the half-pound can of Vogue towards him.

"One time I remember, Ol Antoine says to me, he says, 'Smith, he's like big tree, out on the grass, when him sun is hot.'"

Smith put the tobacco can down on the table and looked at it and at his hand, which covered its top. "He says that about me, eh? I'm like the shade of a tall tree?"

Norah was almost laughing out loud when she put the whole eighty dollars into Smith's hand. "Go on," she said. "Fire up the old truck and you and Young Alexander go in to the Lake and bail him out. There's enough for the mower parts there, too. Go on, you got to get the parts. Go on. You might as well get it over with."

"I spose you're right," he said. "Okay, Young Alexander. You and me will go to Williams Lake and we will get Ol Antoine out of the jail, and ship him off to some other jail, and the Queen will order that I be sold for baloney for murdering Haines, but that is okay, I guess. Where's my best shirt, Norah?"

"I go wait for you that truck now," said Young Alexander.

"Yep, Aleksanter. Okay. I come out any minute now and we fire up that old truck," said Smith.

He shaved and put on his hand-tooled riding boots that were normally reserved for stampede time. He could find no jeans unbleached but he found a pair without holes in the knees or seat. Then he put on the whipcord shirt that had the many buttons, each of which glowed like a small moonstone, and Norah brushed all the dust from his old black hat and put it properly upon his head, flat, with the front brim resting just one inch above the eyebrow.

"You look almost handsome," she said, "Not like a jack pine cowboy at all, but like a Hollywood cowboy."

"I will bust in as fast as the old rig will take me tonight," he said. "I should make it back by day after tomorrow."

As he started for the door she stopped him and handed him another ten. "Smith," she said, "you been going hard. Take this."

"What's that? Where did you get that?"

"Never mind. I had it. When you get to the Lake, find some of your friends and buy them a drink. I guess it wouldn't go far in the bar, but you could buy for them in the beer parlour. Or you could get two bottles of rye and have them up to your hotel room."

He held the ten-dollar bill in his hand for a second or two, looking at it. "There are times that you amaze me," he said. The ten was new and crisp. He folded it two times, streaking the folds with his hard thumbnail. He put the little square of paper in the left-hand breast pocket of the shirt and buttoned the pearly button over it. "Thanks, Norah," he said.

In the old pickup, with the engine that sounded like a bagful of hammers, Young Alexander greeted him in good spirits. Young Alexander did not carry grudges.

They rattled out through the corral gate with the engine full bore and on the log bridge over the creek Smith bounced her so hard that it seemed all four wheels had lifted from the floury dust of the trail. Young Alexander's hat came off against the windshield. He found it again on the floor and put it back on his head and grinned. He was once a rodeo rider who had won money at Calgary.

"You almost lose him first jump, Smith," he said. "I think might be you got them stirrups too long."

"I will make up points by hard spurring," said Smith.

And Ol Antoine

The effect of Norah's actions on the course of
these events cannot be entirely apparent, any
more than those of the several other people
involved. All made their small contribution to
the process of inevitability. But certainly she
was a disruptive influence at this point in
time, because to tell Smith to go out and have
a drink was not only unnecessary but also unprecedented. It threw him off balance. He was
like the saddle-bronc rider who comes out of the
chute all over the horse, hollering, "Getting
bucked off? Hell! I never got on him."

In Smith's youth the drink had been Peaches
Wine. It was a natural fermentation of sugar and
water, flavoured with canned peaches. It was
brewed in a warm corner of the kitchen, the
stove being kept aglow through the long watches
of the night so that the usual nightly chill did
not settle in the cabin. After ten days it was
ready for drinking or bottling. Some said that
there had never been a batch of Peaches Wine
bottled in the history of Namko.

Although legend has come to attribute to
Peaches Wine a power greater than schnapps or

slivovitz or other exotic drinks, the truth is that Peaches Wine probably never exceeded eighteen per cent alcohol by volume. There are stronger fortified wines. But Peaches Wine was usually drunk rapidly, within the confines of small hot cabins, by eager men and after long periods of drought. Accordingly its effect was out of all proportion to its strength, and long-time residents swore that the stuff had something to it not yet discovered by the engineers of such better-known operations as Seagrams and Gooderham Worts.

Sometimes a distillation of Peaches Wine was achieved. A fully matured ten-day-brew was placed in a large pot upon the top of the stove. A miniature three-legged stool was set on the bottom of the pot with a cup or some other small container on top of it. The lid of the pot was then put on upside down. Snow or ice could be used to cool the lid of the pot. As the alcohol simmered off the wine it would condense upon the lower face of the lid, run to the lowest point and then drip into the cup provided there. It was a slow and inefficient process and one seldom used.

Over the years the outer halo of prosperity had spread over the cattle ranges and ranchers and even impoverished Indians came to afford whisky. Whisky was thus a symbol of health and wealth in an operation. It was admired as well as drunk. It was similar to what Catholics call the state of grace, respectable but seldom attainable.

Smith's drinking had included richer fare during the period of his disagreement with Hitler. He had drunk the fine Highland malt with the sheep-herder father of a girl named Flora Macdonald. He had retched up sour calvados in Normandy and there had his head held by a girl named Marie, or something. Yet for all this, drinking played a small part in his life and when he did drink he did so with little style.

He drank at Namko's two main social events, the Cattlemen's Association meeting in fall and the stampede in summer, because it was considered churlish to be stone cold sober at such events. But if he drank much it made him hungry and when he ate it made him sleepy and he seldom attained the high euphoria that Morton Dilloughby could reach after a single sniff of the cork. Norah had once asked him why it was that drinking never elevated him to the status of being the life of the party and he had answered that it did. There was a period, he said, between his first few drinks and the onset of hunger in which he was a gay and witty fellow, but unfortunately with him that period lasted for only about seventy-five seconds.

In the matter of a trip to distant Williams Lake, the customs of drinking and finance were mingled in visiting cattlemen in curious ways.

In the normal course of events, Smith would not have carried actual money in to the Lake with him for this purpose. He might have had a few ten-dollar bills in his shirt pocket, but these would have been for hotel room, entertainment or impulse buying. The mower parts would have been charged or, in the language of the country, put on his jawbone. Like most ranchers, he paid his bills once a year. If funds should fail him during his stay he would cash a cheque at the bank. On this visit, however, he could cash no cheques and, having made arrangements with his banker to discuss the financial position in October when the beef drive came in, he saw no need to see that gentleman on this occasion. In the fall, when he would bring in his cattle, including those survivors held over from the previous year when the price had dropped to a sickening low, he would have enough to pay the banker off—all the money he owed him, possibly—and would be in a position to negotiate for new money to operate during the next twelve-month period. Ken Larsen, Namko's most prosperous rancher, would then no doubt be with him as well as Frenchie Bernard and others. In the flush of his probable prosperity Ken would purchase a whole case of whisky, one bottle of which he would take first to the bank manager's office. The whisky was not for the manager's consumption. It was Ken's going-home bottle. He knew of no safer place to cache it than in the drawer of a bank manager's desk. New bank managers at the National were sometimes quite upset by this, but it was the custom.

Then the end of the ranches' financial year would be celebrated in appropriate manner.

But none of these habits fitted a trip to the Lake in the blaze of August, during haying time. Smith had little or no interest in meeting friends—who was going to be in town at this time of year, anyway?—and it had been so many weeks or months since he'd tasted alcohol that waiting another couple of months would not much matter. His intention was to get in, get out and go home. And yet Norah had told him he should pause for a drink.

There can be no doubt that her influence was disruptive.

The course of events was this: Smith and Young Alexander rolled down the long hill out of Chilcotin, past the Holding Ground and into the town at four A.M. At four-ten A.M. Smith let Young Alexander out of the truck at the Indian camp on the stampede grounds, assuring him that all would be made well with Ol Antoine that morning. At four-thirty A.M. he registered at the Lakeview Hotel and there he slept for a few hours. (There is no view of the lake to be had from the Lakeview. It overlooks the railway station, not far from the stockyards. Many ranchers made a habit of staying there.)

Smith rose at nine-thirty A.M., got into his pearly-buttoned shirt and other clothes and dined at a nearby Chinese restaurant on steak and eggs. There had been no one in the lobby he knew and he saw none of his friends in the restaurant or on the street. He decided to stick with his original plan and get out of town in a hurry. At about eleven he would spring Ol Antoine from jail. He would get his mower parts just before the shops closed for the noon hour. He would pay cash for them. He might get out of town as early as three P.M. Should he meet a friend or two he might purchase one bottle of rye, share it with them in his room and then take a short nap. Then about eight P.M. he would make a Hudson's Bay start for Namko, pausing for a partial night's sleep about one hundred miles west of town. Whichever the case, he did not intend to buy the new rifle he had wanted for some time. It was an admirable schedule, particularly for a man who scarcely understood the word.

At ten-thirty on the sidewalk outside the café he met Boots Maclean, a small rancher from the Likely district, and was prevailed upon to join Boots for a beer. After steak and eggs Smith had little room in his narrow gut for beer, but he was anxious to hear about Boots' new stud and Boots was anxious to discuss the animal.

Boots had bought a Tennessee Walking Horse stallion at an auction in Puyallup, Washington, the price being suspiciously low, and word of this purchase had spread slowly across the land. This was Smith's first opportunity to get a first-hand report.

"He's meaner'n catshit," reported Boots. "Just the way I like them."

For the next twenty minutes he expounded upon the merits of Tennessee Walking Horses. Smith sat with a hand clasped around the chaste waist of a twenty-cent beer glass and listened. He intended to offer some of his own thoughts about horses when Boots ran out of words.

Nearby sat a man whose name is lost to us. Whence he came, none knew and where he was going he knew not himself. He was very drunk. Not drunk again; it was the same old drunk that he had been on for a week. This man was a very deceptive drinker in that the more he consumed the more sober he appeared to become. Also, no matter how drunk he might be, he shaved each morning and kept his overalls neat. But beneath the calm exterior of a man apparently devoted to the sober career of garage mechanic or sawmill hand there lurked a strong passion for action as well as for drink. After his first glass of beer he stood at his table, holding his empty glass in his hand and looked across the room to the man who stood behind the beer parlour taps. He waited until he caught the tapman's eye. Then he held the empty glass high and said, "Waiter, this glass don't work any more." He then threw it at the tapman, who ducked. The glass shattered against the wall.

"You are now on the Siwash list," said the tapman, rising again from behind the counter. He came forward to throw out the man in overalls.

There was a small scuffle, to which Smith gave only cursory attention. These things happened. It was none of his business.

He was alone at his table at the moment, Boots having made a trip to the toilet.

Although he was too drunk to know what day it was, the man in overalls was surprisingly strong. The table overturned while the tapman was attempting to get a hammerlock on him to escort him to the door. Smith was considering that he should perhaps give the tapman a hand. He did not like noise in the morning, either. At that point the drunk lurched towards Smith and grabbed his shirt in hands strong as pliers. The regular hotel waiter, who weighed two hundred pounds and sometimes made money in professional wrestling, came into the beer parlour just as Smith, the drunk and the tapman went down in a heap on the floor.

The waiter was not the brightest of men but he knew a fight when he saw one, and he was quite sure the Lakeview's tapman was not a willing participant. He collared Smith and the drunk, knocked their heads together, dragged them to the swinging doors and flung them forth into the morning.

It took some time for the tapman to explain to the bouncer that the cowboy hadn't done anything, so far as he knew, yet.

The drunk's head had proved harder than Smith's. He had scarcely hit the sidewalk when he got to his feet, spoke briefly and pungently about everybody, then walked away in drunken solemnity, leaving Smith to try to lie down without holding on to anything.

There was lightning playing behind Smith's eyes, yellow and sometimes orange, and he lay on the sidewalk for a minute or more with his face turned to the sky. His shirt was ripped from armpit to breakfast-time and beer had spilled on him. He was lying there when the Supreme Court judge who was conducting the Assizes came out of the Lakeview and started towards the courthouse.

It was the first time that Smith and the judge had met.

The judge looked at him, stepped over him and made his way up the street. He was occupied with an Indian murder trial that day. Smith was vomiting up his one glass of beer as the judge departed. The bump on his head seemed to have affected his digestion.

The whole matter was quickly settled, of course. Boots brought him inside. The tapman fanned him. The bouncer apologized all to hell and the manager dashed down from the lobby to offer apologies and anything else that might seem to work. As the town stopped spinning, Smith, who was a reasonable man, agreed that these things happened in the best-run of hotels. He accepted the price of a new shirt from the management, put the one he wore together with some pins and at eleven-thirty A.M. he went up to the skookum house to retrieve Ol Antoine. He was almost on schedule.

Oliver Street was becoming glazed in plastic tile, and neons, burning even by day, flickered above the stores. The streets were filled with large cars. The town was about ready for its first supermarket. It was a noisier place than he remembered it, for that time of day, and he did not recognize one face. His head ached.

It had been his intention to speak sternly to the police, explaining that their prisoner, "Abraham," was not Abraham but a harmless old stick from the Namko Country named Ol Antoine. But there was only one very young constable behind the desk and he sensed that the time spent in getting such a youth to release a prisoner was not worth the effort. So he paid "Abraham's" full ten-dollar fine, even though Abraham had only the rest of the day to serve, and when Ol Antoine was brought to the office, blinking in the sunlight, Smith spoke to him rapidly in Chinook: "Neseyeka klatawa, Ol Antoine."

"Okay," said Ol Antoine, "we go."

He took Ol Antoine out the back door and down the street towards the truck. They were almost there before the Indian realized that they were leaving the courthouse, not walking to it. He turned and started back up the street.

"I go now that place and talk for Kabriel," he said.

"You stay right with me and we go home in

104

the truck," said Smith, but Ol Antoine kept walking the ball-and-heel walk of a man used to moccasins. Smith followed and got in front of him. Then the old man had to stop.

"Ol Antoine, you keep out of that court."

"I tell Kabriel I come talk for him that place."

"You make cultus wawa in that court, you will be in real trouble. You understand that thing? Real trouble. More bigger trouble than you had already. You have got nothing to tell those people about the Haines murder."

The old man did not answer. Smith continued.

"I do not know much, Ol Antoine, but I know a few things. One thing I learned long time ago —keep out of courts, hospitals and, if possible, the army. Come on, we go back to Namko now."

"It's okay, I kess. Walter Charlie, he's 'nterpreter that place. Talks real koot, I think."

"Walter Charlie *hell*!"

"He's shmart, Walter Charlie. Talks real koot."

"Yeah, but spose he don't talk real good. Spose he fools you. Maybe he don't fix it up, your talk, when you talk that place. Might be he fools you. He already got that reward money, ent it? Ol Antoine, you listen while I talk to you in the head. Do you really trust Walter Charlie?"

"He's Intian, ent it?"

"Well now, is he? I just wonder. Personally, I would say that Walter Charlie is at least one-quarter white."

"Ent anypoty all the way good, I spose," said Ol Antoine, and he stepped around Smith and kept walking up the street.

Smith laughed. "By damn, old man," he said, "I do like your style."

He followed him again.

He stopped him once more half-way up the courthouse steps.

"Ol Antoine," he said, "you come away to Namko with me. This is not a town for people like you and me any more, Ol Antoine. It is not a place for cowboys and Indians now. It is a businessman's town now. You come back to Namko with me."

"I break that quarter horse for you real quick, after couple days' little time."

"Ol Antoine, I do not care about that quarter horse. Not really. You just come back and we will forget about the horse. In fact, I tell you what we will do. We will go on a hunt." He looked at the sky, much as Macdonald Lasheway had looked at it a few days before and he said, in much the same tones as Lasheway had used, "This weather is goin to hold all right. The haying can wait for a week or ten days."

He touched Ol Antoine on the forearm. "This is what we will do. We will take two saddlehorses, one packhorse, two bed rolls, one rifle and one shaker of salt. That is all, horses, a rifle and a shaker of salt. We will go up into the hills with the crust on the top of them, and we will kill ourselves a caribou. Then we will make camp, and we will sit there and eat that caribou until it is all gone, and we will tell wonderful stories to one another."

He thought for a moment that he had him, but Ol Antoine began to talk in Chilcotin.

He took some more slow steps towards the courthouse door.

Smith tried once more, in Chinook. It is only a jargon but when carried lightly at the front of the mouth and half sung it can be musical. Smith carried his voice up and down as he spoke it, like the line of the hills beyond Namko.

"Ol Antwyne, neseyeka klatawa, Ol Antwyne. Neseyeka klatawa, kopa siaaaaaah sahkalie stone illahie."

Ol Antoine looked for a moment towards the hills that they could not see and then he turned and walked into the courthouse.

"Go, then," said Smith. "Go, you stubborn old son of a bitch."

The Judge

The Williams Lake courthouse, two storeys high and square as the cross, was built in the 1920s when the Cariboo had experienced a sudden rush of blood to the head caused by a powerful feeling of prosperity. It may be that it was built ahead of its time. In those years there were not many laws. However, the few they had, the people broke; it was felt that the structure was indeed justified. Of course, the times were good. In those years it was believed that the stock market, beef prices, wages, debts and government hand-outs could increase to infinity without let or hindrance. The money supply was endless, the proof being that the population was increasing every year. It was shortly to be arranged that everybody should become healthy and wise, and there was never going to be another severe winter. Odd, the way people thought in those days.

The Williams Lake courthouse compared to Vancouver's much as is suggested by the politicians' joke about the Pacific Great Eastern Railway—not as long as the CPR, but just as wide. There were no stone lions on the Williams Lake

courthouse steps. Even the steps were of wood.
A sign at the door said WIPE YOUR BOOTS OFF.
The colour of the Williams Lake courthouse
was not grime grey, like Vancouver's, but grime
mustard. The paint for it had been chosen by a
decorator then recently come from the mustard-
plaster district of Bavaria, specifically München,
home of mad King Ludwig, who apparently
favoured that shade. Such is the proof of the
power of artistic impulse, spanning continents
and oceans to link Bavaria with the Cariboo.

Within the clapboard walls of the Williams
Lake courthouse were repeated in form if not
in substance most of the features of the big
city's justice dispensary. In the big city the
floors were of red tile, here they were grey
battleship linoleum. Vancouver courthouse had
corridors. Williams Lake had hallways. Both
buildings contained many offices full of lead-
faced civil servants, but at Williams Lake these
were people in their sixties instead of in their
forties.

The courtroom was also considerably smaller
than any one of Vancouver's, though just as just,
of course. In Williams Lake the jurymen sat on
bar chairs beside the windows that face on
Oliver Street and they had been known to rise
from these chairs to watch something interesting
on the street outside, even though the court
might be in session at such a time. There were
three doors. One was for the judge, one for
lawyers and officials, policemen and prisoners,

109

and the third for spectators. Spectators were separated from the main scene of action by a low railing. There was a small witness box, another small prisoner's box, a table and the Bench.

The Williams Lake courthouse has other features than clapboards and paint from mad King Ludwig. It has also many small offices, old desks, dust and rats big as badgers.

(On consideration, it must be said that there are a lot of damn lies in the above. The courthouse is pretty much Mid-Thirties CPR Railway Station Architecture. Also, the Cariboo Assizes are not held in Williams Lake. Some years ago, when the Assizes were being held in unfortunate conjunction with the annual stampede, a Supreme Court justice of B.C. said to his sheriff, "Mr. Sheriff, I think your jury is drunk," to which the sheriff replied, "I am God-damned sure they're drunk. We lock them up in their hotel room every night but their friends are sorry for them because they're locked up during stampede and they pass them bottles down from the roof, on ropes." Shortly after this the Assizes were transferred seventy miles up the highway to Quesnel, a town of notable sobriety.)

At the moment this building contained several characters of note. The judge was one. He was a mixed man. He had been a politician who had become a political liability, fit only for minor diplomatic posting abroad or for the Senate. At the time that his exclusion from the political apparatus became necessary, neither of these areas of the national life had any vacancies. It was finally decided that he should be elevated to the Bench, the decision being made by a typical political hierarchy, composed of a high-society White Anglo-Saxon Protestant who had been cashiered from the militia for stealing from the mess fund, another less noticeable man who had married well, a loan shark and two faceless young men who wore Homburg hats.

This judge proceeded to astonish and dismay his peers by exhibiting a native inflexibility, an occasional stupidity and an infuriating mixture of compassion, brilliance and exotic flashes of emotion that make a man simply impossible. Even those confident of their own unshakable righteousness came to be fearful of the day when they might be thrust in front of him. He had been, at this time, a County Court judge in Kootenay for thirty years and, by some miscalculation of the Justice Department, a justice of the Supreme Court of British Columbia for five. This was his first Assizes in Cariboo.

He had been born a devout Christian of Baptist and something like Quaker origins and had some years previously turned agnostic—well known to be the worst kind. However, he had told no one of his conversion, not even his wife, with whom he went each Sunday that he was in Vancouver to the First Baptist Church of Kerrisdale. In that, as in other things, he was outwardly a man of the highest probity. He drank

nothing stronger than table wine, raised dachs-
hunds, and read at least one hundred and fifty
new books every year. He slept with his window
open and exhausted much of his salary with
secret charities to the bafflement of his family
and his investment counsellors.

Even when not in the scarlet robes of the
Supreme Court there was something forbidding
in his dress. He wore suits that were dark, with
vests, and black boots with calfskin uppers,
which he shined himself each morning down in
his basement beside the coal stoker of his old
furnace. His face was plank-like, crossed by rim-
less glasses and shaven to the quick.

To see him upon the bench was to be re-
minded of a chiffonier, made in the full flower-
ing of the Victorian age. It was easy to believe
that he also had ball-and-claw feet.

Behind the doors of this chiffonier there lay
in the aromatic dust all sorts of impulses: to
whoredom and tyranny and the cold adaman-
tine luxury of pride; to warmth and the scent of
lilac and the sweet words of poets, to God and
to things too dark to be mentioned. He was, in
short, very much like other men, but more
prominent.

In the British House of Lords, or as a judge in
Texas, he might have given free play to his
eccentricities and by that means have adopted
the protective colouration of normality. In the
Canadian courts, which did not look kindly
upon human impulse, he found it necessary to

draw around him the cloak of that austere tradition of dignity. It had preserved many such a judge before him, and would probably serve for his lifetime.

About the only thing that broke through, as a rule, was his passion for nicotine. Sometimes when a case drew long he would reach inside the wide scarlet front of his robe, extract a cigar from a pocket, break off the end, place that end in his mouth with a movement like that of a man covering a yawn, and then chew it. He would chew it, slowly, and then swallow. Swallow all of it.

The Crown Counsel was a man of great ability. He was then about fifty or fifty-five and adorned with a Toronto Conservative moustache, a crisp new gown and an old purple QC's bag, which he dragged about after him in ostentatious carelessness, as if laying track for hounds. He was the owner of a colonial-style home set in forty acres of expensively watered lawn outside Quesnel. He had three race horses and a three-point-eight Jag and a wife who could still dye her hair pink and avoid censure. For his work, he drove a three-year-old Ford, standard. Ranchers mistrusted affluence, and he had many of their accounts. It was popularly though incorrectly believed that he had inherited three ranch estates from clients.

His first Assizes had been a joy. He knew the publicity value for a clever man, and he knew himself to be clever. Such was his success from that beginning that he continued to accept the chore of Crown Counsel once every three years. He abandoned more lucrative practice for this work at these intervals but did it, out of a sense of gratitude, or duty, or possibly superstition. Whether turning out a chess set on his basement lathe, or prosecuting a grubby rape case, he liked to do a thing well and he did not spare effort nor count his cost nor his profit in doing so.

He was somewhat irritated about the case immediately preceding Gabriel Jimmyboy's. It had been the most intriguing one of these Assizes, far more so than Gabriel's. A cowboy of the huge Burned Lake Ranch had been found lying in the sagebrush beside the Little Fort trail. He had been shot, strangled and beaten, but was still alive and continued so. Three of his fellow cowboys from the Burned Lake Ranch had been charged with attempting his murder.

Their defence had been simple. Their unfortunate friend, they all said, had had too much to drink. This made him remorseful. While all four men were driving home in the pickup truck on the Little Fort road, their friend had pulled the deer gun off the back of the seat and tried to kill himself, narrowly missing his brains.

Quickly sensing that all was not well, the four cowboys had got out of the truck and the three unshot ones had attempted to give first aid to the wounded man. He resisted them. They had to choke him and hit him a few times with a rock to make him relax sufficiently to receive first aid treatment. Having determined that he wasn't very badly hurt after all, they had all driven away in the pickup to seek more medical aid, leaving their companion resting in the sagebrush.

Somewhat to the surprise of the Crown, the victim corroborated all this. He had been drinking, he said, at the time, but the explanation sounded reasonable to him. The other cowboys were all his friends, he said, and he wished that the police would not get mixed up in things like this.

Acquittal had been prompt.

It was another jury that sat to decide the matter between the Queen and Gabriel Jimmyboy. Its composition was usual: ranchers predominated. There were also a couple of merchants, retired, and other middle-aged and elderly men of grey hue and undetermined origin. They were all wearing ties, some for the first time in years. It was not a happy jury.

The Crown had presented all its evidence in a single day and it was clear, concise and apparently comprehensive evidence, quite sufficient proof that Canada would be a better place without Gabriel. The defence had presented nothing but a series of adjournments that were now in their second day. During this period the jurymen had had to be locked away from newspapers, radios and the public lest their minds be polluted by the sort of gossip that they had been listening to right up to the moment of their being impanelled. Almost all this time they had spent locked in their steaming-hot hotel rooms, where the ranchers discussed the marvellous haying weather that was being missed. Occasionally the sheriff led them up the street to the courthouse, where they heard the defence lawyer explain yet again why he could not proceed with his case just yet.

The ceiling of the courtroom was low. The room was almost as hot as their hotel room. In addition to judge and jury, Crown Counsel and Defence Counsel, spectators and the unspeaking and unsmiling Gabriel Jimmyboy, there were also in that little room a stenographer, a court clerk, a sheriff and two policemen.

One was a corporal who had served more than twenty-five years on the northern coast of B.C., sometimes acting as a policeman, sometimes as a judge and often as a friend to the people who lived in his large district. He had never been particularly popular with his superiors, but when the provincial police department was incorporated into the Royal Canadian Mounted Police and there was a lofty headquarters staff in Ottawa, the home and heart of all loftiness, his manner became insufferable.

Once, in writing a report, he had injected one of the commonly used Chinook words, hyack, for hurry up. This word being questioned, he had written, "Who is the horse's ass who doesn't

116

know that word?" The horse's ass who didn't know was a commissioned officer who prided himself upon his knowledge of the north country. At the time of the Jimmyboy murder trial the corporal had recently been transferred to Williams Lake from the north coast. It was unlikely that he would rise above corporal before his retirement date.

The other policeman was a young man who preferred highway patrol to this sort of work.

"My Lord," said Samuels, "I find myself in a most difficult position."

"Again?" said Crown Counsel, in a voice low enough that it was not heard, officially.

"I'm more sorry than I can say about the inconvenience to this court, and to these gentlemen of the jury, but I am afraid that I find myself obliged to ask for a further adjournment."

The gentlemen of the jury looked bleak.

Crown Counsel rose, and Samuels reluctantly sat.

"Surely, Milord," said the bland and fluent Mr. Edwards, "surely my learned friend is not going to impose further upon the time of this court and the time of these jurymen?"

Samuels said, "My Lord, I am awaiting a very important witness for my case."

"We were awaiting him yesterday," said the judge.

"I fully appreciate that, My Lord, and I am very sorry."

117

Crown Counsel stood again. "Milord, may I make a statement as to the Crown's position?"

"Proceed."

"The Crown has no interest in this case, except that all the facts, all the facts, Milord, should be placed before these gentlemen of the jury. Facts brought forward by the defence equally with those brought forward by the Crown."

"Yes, yes," said the judge, who could be expected to know this.

"But, My Lord, there are limits to which the services of these good citizens of the jury should not be strained. This jury has now been locked up for a full additional twenty-four hours, an unnecessary twenty-four hours, awaiting the arrival of this important witness, this nameless, faceless and apparently so utterly important witness of my learned friend. At least he might have brought forward other witnesses while this key figure was being found, wherever he may be."

Edwards knew that Samuels had no other witness, as did the judge, but Samuels did not know enough to spit out the hook. "We have no other witness, My Lord," Samuels said.

"Then," said Crown Counsel, "if my learned friend had but one witness and this one of such unique importance, he should have been produced here on time. Many of these gentlemen of the jury are ranchers, My Lord, and this is haying time."

The judge had listened to Crown Counsel rasp the jurymen's nerves twice the previous afternoon, and it was beginning to irritate him, much as he admired Edwards' fluent performance. "I do not know what haying has to do with the Crown's anxiety to get all the evidence forward," he said.

"My client is on trial for his life," said Samuels.

"Yes," said Crown Counsel, "for his life, and if there are witnesses of such importance, then my learned friend should have enough concern for this matter to produce those witnesses on time, here, when they are called. I appreciate Your Lordship's remarks, naturally, that the private affairs of these gentlemen of the jury are of no overwhelming importance in a capital case . . ."

"Yes, yes, yes," said the judge, "I fully appreciate the Crown's position. Thank you, Mr. Edwards. Mr. Samuels."

Samuels rose. Edwards sat, hiding a smile.

"I must say, Mr. Samuels," said the judge, "I am totally unable to understand why this witness cannot be produced, and none of your explanations yesterday or today have relieved my mind."

"My Lord, he was told to be here yesterday."

"Told, Mr. Samuels, told! Why was there no request that a subpoena be served upon this man?"

"Precisely," said Crown Counsel. "Why was he not subpoenaed?"

119

"The amplification of my remarks by the Crown is not required," said His Lordship, and Crown Counsel, having reinforced his point, apologized and sat down.

"Well, My Lord, it is very difficult to explain the difficulties involved in dealing with a witness across such wide distances as are involved. He is across the Chilcotin, and beyond the roads also, I understand. . . ." He faltered, and stopped.

"I now find myself in a most difficult position," said His Lordship.

Samuels said, "My Lord, may I consult my client?"

Crown Counsel rose to say, "Another adjournment!" and the jury almost came to their feet with him.

"I will just speak to him in the hallway, My Lord. There may be some way out of the difficulty."

"Very well, Mr. Samuels."

The young policeman took Gabriel out into the hall and Samuels followed, while the jury, left in the relaxed courtroom, gave off a sullen murmur.

The young policeman walked a few feet down the hall, his boots and the boards each making their own squeaks. He clasped his hands behind his back and stared at a painting of the first German gas attack upon the Canadians at Ypres. At the stairway's landing was Walter Charlie, the interpreter, smoking a cigarette.

"Gabriel, haven't you any idea where Ol Antoine may be?"

There was no response.

"Did he leave the Reserve? Do you know if he is on his way here?"

"Is there no one we could ask who could tell us where Ol Antoine might be? Could I phone somewhere near to Namko Reserve? Is there anyone who might know?"

"He says he comes here, talks for me," said Gabriel.

"Well, tell me, what is the evidence that he is going to give? You never told me, Gabriel, and Ol Antoine couldn't understand what I asked him the one time I did see him."

"He comes talk for me here."

"Gabriel, there is something that you have never understood about you and me. You can tell me anything. Anything at all. Good or bad. I am not the court. I am not a policeman, Gabriel. I am you. In law, Gabriel, you and I are one person. We are the same person. Can't you understand that?"

"Sure too bad, they hang you, too."

"Well, if you insist on treating me as an enemy there just isn't anything much that I can do for you, Gabriel."

"I think Ol Antwyne comes pretty quick," said Gabriel, looking down the stairs at Ol Antoine and Walter Charlie. Ol Antoine spoke briefly to Walter, who returned one very short burst of words, too faint to be heard.

"You have been saying for days he would be here pretty quick."

"He comes quick," said Gabriel, more loudly, as Ol Antoine made his way up the stairs.

"Who is that?" said Samuels.

"I say it's Ol Antwyne," said Gabriel, loudly. He found this young man quite annoying at times. "I told you he comes talk for me this place."

A conversation with Ol Antoine was no more enlightening this time than previously. Samuels decided to put him on the stand in his natural state. He could almost feel the sweaty irritation of the jurymen through the walls of the court-room.

Joseph of the Nez Percé

The air was wet as well as hot and only a thunderstorm could free the town from its weight that day and the thunderhead was not even building yet. Primitive men would rest in such oppressive heat, confident that the great lightning god would soon set fire to the air and make it clean and fresh for them again, but civilized men used such days to break up partnerships, to commit suicide or to kill small children with automobiles.

Samuels would put Ol Antoine on the stand, for better or worse, now. He had done his best. It had not been very good, but it had been his best. Nobody could take that away from him. Of course nobody was likely to try, either.

They all went into the courtroom and Samuels began a long, profuse apology, which the judge cut short.

"I believe this witness will need an interpreter," Samuels then said.

"They always do," said the Crown Counsel, just loudly enough to be heard by the jury.

Meanwhile, Smith had come into the courthouse. He entered, he told himself, only to pick

123

up a map in the land commissioner's office. He had done all he could for that crazy old bugger and he was not going to do one thing more. He stood for a long time at the desk but all the people in the office were writing reports to Victoria and nobody looked up at him. So he walked out, and this time he noticed Walter Charlie enjoying his cigarette. A little man began swinging a hammer at the bottom of Smith's throat. He walked up to the landing and stood beside Walter.

"Walter," he said, "did you steer that old man into the wrong court? So he would get thrown into the skookum house? Was that your doing?"

"Me, I mind my own business, Smith. Sure seems good idea, I think."

"Never mind the funny talk. You listen to me. You got that money. You see you do a good job for that old man when he's on that witness stand."

"I don't 'nderstant what you're talkin about, Smith. I ain't so shmart, I guess. I don't 'nderstant."

"You understand, all right, and you hear me: you do what you're sposed to do."

"I'm 'nterpreter that court."

Smith forced himself to use a softer tone. "Walter," he said, "who is going to help Indians in this world if Indians don't help one another? Ol Antoine's one of your own people. He's Indian, like you, Chilcotin."

124

"You figure Ol Antoine's Chilcotin, eh Smith?" said Walter.

"Certainly. What do you mean?"

"Funny thing," said Walter, who was enjoying this as some men do brandy, "all that time you live there, you don't know Ol Antwyne's a breed." And then, lightly, "You never hear Ol Antwyne he's quarter Nez Percé?"

The policeman called and Walter went quickly up the stairs. Smith followed him and went through the door into the spectators' section and sat in the back row of chairs.

"You are still under oath, Mr. Interpreter," said the Court Clerk, and Walter nodded his head in agreement. They swore Ol Antoine to tell the truth, the whole truth and nothing but the truth, so help him God, and he agreed to do that.

Ol Antoine had seated himself in the witness box, without waiting for an invitation to do so by the court. It was not a very big box, but he was so small that it seemed big. He had a green nylon kerchief, very dirty, tied around his neck. Thin white hair fell over his forehead and his ears. The jury were close enough that they could see the dozen or so long white hairs that grew from his chin. As a young man he had shaved by pulling them out, but now that he was an old man he did not shave any more.

"You've got a lot of ground to make up with that witness, Samuels," whispered the Crown Counsel.

125

"You're telling me!" the younger man answered. He was ruffling a few papers on the table before him. They had nothing to do with Ol Antoine, but it made him feel better to pretend that they did.

Samuels walked over to stand beside the jury. Walter stood beside the witness, hands behind his back, shifting back and forth from the balls of his feet to the heels. He was supposed to address his translation to judge and jury, but frequently did so to the spectators. He enjoyed this job. In interpretation his voice altered from the normal. It became quite loud and distinct, though also flat and unemotional.

Samuels said, "Now, Ol Antoine. You know what it is that we are dealing with here today."

Walter repeated this, loudly, in Chilcotin, not addressing the witness but turning his face to one far corner of the courtroom ceiling, projecting his voice there as if for the pleasure of seeing if it would bounce. Ol Antoine answered in the same language, speaking to the dusty floor between his feet.

Walter spoke English at the corner of the ceiling.

"He says I am going to talk to the Indian peoples who are here."

A piece of Samuels' liver flaked off, but he kept his voice clear, bright and friendly. "Yes, of course, everybody in this courtroom is going to hear what he says. But it is to these gentlemen of the jury and to His Lordship that we want

Ol Antoine to speak on this matter. Now, Ol
Antoine, I want you to take your time and tell
this court, these gentlemen in the jury and His
Lordship everything that you know about this
matter."

The interpretation ran back and forth,
Walter speaking to the sky and the old man to
the earth.

Then Walter spoke clear English.

"I will tell the peoples about the time when
I was a young man with Chief Joseph, and we
fought the white savages in Montana."

There was a murmur of laughter from the
jury. Possibly the day was not to be completely
wasted if there were to be a little humour in it.
Some of the Indian spectators also laughed.

"Order," said the sheriff, speaking to the
spectators.

"Your Lordship," said Samuels, "I think
perhaps the interpreter has not made himself
entirely clear."

Crown Counsel rose. "The interpreter has
made himself perfectly well understood by nine
other Chilcotins in these Assizes."

"Do you wish a second interpreter brought in,
Mr. Samuels?" said the judge.

"My Lord, and gentlemen of the jury, I was
not criticizing the ability of this interpreter. It
is just that these surroundings are a little strange
to my witness and possibly I have not made
myself entirely clear to him. Old Antoine, now
you understand that what we are concerned with

here is the trial of the prisoner, this man, Gabriel Jimmyboy, who is charged with murder? And it is about this matter of the murder that we want to know what you can tell us to help us."

The interpretation was quite lengthy this time and so was the reply. First Walter spoke, then Ol Antoine spoke, then Walter spoke, this time directly to him, and Ol Antoine answered with a hundred words or more.

"He says yes," said Walter.

"Yes, of course," said Samuels. "He was just a trifle confused for a moment. Now, Old Antoine, will you just take your time and tell us, in your own words, everything that you know about this matter concerning Gabriel Jimmyboy?"

When the English came back it was, "I remember that day Chief Joseph talks to us. I remember that day very well."

The laughter was such that the sheriff had to stand and rap on his desk beside the judge, shouting, "Order. Order in court." Even Ol Antoine noticed it. He raised his head, looked at Walter and spoke to him, at length.

"He says," said Walter, "that it is for me to tell the white peoples whatever it is they want to hear."

"Order," cried the sheriff. "Order in the court." But almost everybody was laughing, none more than the jury, and the laughter subsided only slowly.

Walter was the only man who noticed Smith,

who leaned forward in his seat at the back of the room and said in a low and very clear voice, "Walter, I am going to beat the living Jesus out of you for that."

And to that, Walter smiled, and if this whole business were to be summed up in two words, those would be the words: Walter smiled.

He smiled at Smith, secure on his side of the low railing that separated official people from the ordinary kind.

Smith knew that if he were going to live with himself afterwards he would have to do something. He placed his hat on the chair. He even paused to flick a piece of ash from the crown with his finger. Then he walked slowly forward, saying, "Well, then, I will do it right here and now."

The young policeman who sat beside the prisoner's box faced the front of the courtroom, so he could not see him, and the corporal did not notice him until Smith was stepping over the railing, still looking directly at Walter, saying, "I been planning this for a long time."

"Here, here," said the corporal, rising and pushing the palm of his hand in Smith's direction. "You can't come in here."

"It is all right," said Smith. "It's not you I'm after. It is that Siwash bastard there." He stepped past the man.

Because his manner was so mild the corporal was still slow to move, but he reached Smith a few feet from Walter and put a hand on his arm. "You can't come in here," he said.

"Take your hand off me," said Smith.

The corporal grabbed him and Smith broke loose. Walter had stepped behind the counsel table. Smith went right over it with his left fist driving at Walter's mouth. The blow was near the end of his reach but it was enough to split Walter's lip and the blood spurted. Others at the table scattered and it went over. Walter rolled out of reach as both policemen grabbed Smith and that was when the fight began.

His breath came out first in a high whistling shriek and then as he fought he cursed in a high falsetto. He used his feet and his arms and his head and tried to bite and although there were two policemen on him he rolled the whole bundle of them six feet across the floor before they managed to lock his arms and legs and drag him out. Smith's face was covered in blood and he blew bloody foam out of his mouth, having bitten his tongue. The constable's shirt was ripped and the corporal was bowed over with pain from a knee in the groin, but they kept their grip and dragged him down into the cells in the basement.

The judge had watched the courtroom fight with one fist tucked into a cheek, a nervous habit he had that gave him a vicious squint. As Smith's rasping screams and curses faded away into the hall he said, "Mr. Sheriff, you will bring that cowboy before me later in these Assizes."

"Shall we adjourn, My Lord?" said the sheriff.

"What is the feeling of counsel?" said the judge, looking towards Defence Counsel.

"I am uncertain, My Lord," said Samuels.

"If Your Lordship pleases," said Crown Counsel, "surely there has already been too much unnecessary delay and inconvenience for all concerned in this trial. All of these jurymen are busy men. Very busy men."

His Lordship was wearied of cleverness. He had listened to it for thirty years and had found few new variations after the first three. Also, it was a day of sticky heat. "Mr. Edwards," he said, "have you ever considered running for public office?"

"No, My Lord."

"Interesting. Your remarks sometimes remind me of those made on a political platform."

"I assure Your Lordship I have no ambition in regard to politics."

"Pity. The public has quite a treat in store for it if you should change your mind."

Edwards sat down, flushing, and making oath to himself that he would never forgive the judge for those remarks.

"Mr. Samuels," said the judge, "if you feel that an adjournment is now desirable, this court will grant it without any hesitation whatsoever."

The jury were stirring again, but the stale air of the room was not.

"We ask no adjournment, My Lord," said Samuels.

The judge looked down at him and said, softly, "Mr. Samuels."

The lawyer stepped forward and stood beneath him.

"Mr. Samuels, I wonder if I might make a suggestion to you, as an old man speaking to a young man. You know, I have been on the bench in this province for more years than you have been alive." He held up his hand as if to ward off the remarks of Appeal Court judges who so often found him at fault in exchanges such as these. "No slight intended, sir, no slight. Some of us become wiser with age, but some of us just become more hardened in our original follies. But, Mr. Samuels, why don't you just let this old chap here tell his story in his own way, and I will stop it if there is anything improper."

"I thank you, My Lord. I shall ask the witness to proceed."

The judge did not wait for Samuels to act. He turned directly to Ol Antoine.

"Ol Antoine," he said, "there is something that you must understand."

Walter translated. His lip was still bleeding but only slightly, and he was able to mop it occasionally with a handkerchief supplied by the court stenographer.

"You must tell us the things that you know about this case," said the judge. "You must answer the questions that are put to you. It is very important. It is the law."

In translation, the English word law popped in and out of the Chilcotin during the exchange between Walter and Ol Antoine.

Walter recited from Antoine loudly, flat-voiced: "The law is a very hard thing. The law is a very cold thing. I cannot understant the law."

The judge fixed his fist in his cheek and looked at the old man for a moment. Then he said, "Proceed."

Walter translated.

"Proceed, Ol Antoine," said Samuels, and Walter translated that.

There was no response. The old man's head was down and he was looking at the floor of the witness box.

"Tell us now what you know about this matter involving Gabriel Jimmyboy."

Walter spoke this and was not answered. He took one step closer to the witness box, and then another. When finally he stood touching the sides of the box with his side, a low whisper floated up from Ol Antoine.

"I remember that day," translated Walter. "I remember that day very well."

"Yes?" said Samuels, in hope and fear.

"It was in the Bear Paw country in that place Montana. All around us in them snow hills is the white soltiers."

133

Samuels just stood. Some of the jury were beginning to grin again. He tried to tell himself it was better than their frowns.

Ol Antoine addressed his feet some more and the jury murmured in laughter to hear the English words *Chief Joseph* with the unintelligible Chilcotin.

"We all come up that place to hear Chief Joseph," said Walter. "Chief Joseph waits for us on saddle-horse."

Ol Antoine began to stand. It seemed that he was about to depart. But he stopped, not quite erect, keeping his knees bent. He straightened his back and his neck, dropped the right arm straight at his side and held the left slightly forward with the hand clenched. Bobbing gently from the knees, he made a quarter-turn right, turned front, right, then left, and there was a little hum of admiration from the people in the court, for there in front of them was Joseph, sitting one of the great Palouse horses, making his last speech to the Shahapshin while the American regiments waited for them.

He brought up his right hand and shouted.

"Hear me, my chiefs," said Walter.

Just once, at that first sentence, he recovered from his initial surprise and resumed the flat loud, but lifeless voice in which he preferred to translate. But thereafter Walter, too, got caught up in the little drama. His voice came strong or soft as the old man altered his. It was a superb translation because, matching the original as it

134

did, it was possible for the whites to forget that everything was being said twice.

"I am tired of fighting," he said.

"All the old chiefs have been killed by the white savages.

"The chief who led the young men, he has been killed, too.

"We cannot fight any more.

"The peoples are cold ...

"... and we have no blankets.

"The peoples are hungry ...

"... and there is no more meat."

He paused again. Ol Antoine did not look at the Indians in the spectators' benches, nor did they look at him, but their presence now filled the little room.

Life had not been easy for the Chilcotins before the whites arrived in their territory and early settlers reported that they sometimes had to abandon their elderly ones during winter famines. But the years since the whites' arrival had not been kind to them, either. They were a ragged group. Many of them had ceased to do work of any kind and now lived on the government dole. Many had unusual mouths — great bulging gums where flesh had grown over the stumps of teeth that had slowly rotted back to the gum line, aided by a diet heavy in white sugar. One man showed the awkward knobbed knees and the mouth marks of tertiary syphilis.

There were strong faces among them, like that of Macdonald Lasheway, who had once

135

almost succeeded in running a sawmill, and Cyrus James, who could have been yet holding down an excellent job at the Quesnel plywood plant had he not suddenly and without giving notice returned to his Reserve. They had led old Moosemeat Mary Dan there, who was blind. She sat in the second row back, a kerchief covering her face from forehead to the bridge of her nose. She was sitting, as were they all, still but not rigid; attentive, but not responsive.

Ol Antoine then continued.

"The peoples, some of them, have gone away into the snow hills and nobody knows today where they might be.

"It might be that they are freezing to death.

"I want to ride away into the snow hills and look for my childrens. . . . It might be I will find them with the dead."

The old voice had been low; now it came loud and clear again.

"Hear me, my chiefs and my peoples. From where this sun now stands, we will not fight any more."

Then Ol Antoine spoke his last sentence, sat down again and Joseph and the horse were gone. Walter walked away from him.

"I didn't get the reply, Mr. Interpreter," said the court stenographer.

Walter took a breath and let it out in a short sigh. He looked around at the whites, who were rich and smart and called him a dirty cultus Siwash sometimes, and at the Indians for whom

136

he did not have to translate, and then he gave an indirect quotation, in a voice almost offhand.

"He says that now we, all of us peoples, got to go the white man's way."

"Khotsakwaleen," said Ol Antoine, and Walter gave the formal translation. "That is everything that I have to say."

"Well, damn good, I say," said the foreman of the jury.

"Mr. Foreman!" said the sheriff.

"Well, it was: as good a speech as I've ever heard in this courthouse." The foreman was a veteran of jury duty and considered himself to be an expert in such matters. A fellow rancher leaned forward to agree with him. There was an old chap on the Reserve near his place like this one, he said, one of the real skookum tillicums.

Soft voices filled the little room and the sheriff rapped for order again. Samuels started to sit down. He intended to put his head in his hands and possibly weep, or perhaps open his veins with a pocket knife. However, he felt sorry for the old fellow, so he said, gently, "Thank you very much, Ol Antoine, for coming here to talk for your friend, Gabriel Jimmyboy."

The judge smiled.

"No cross-examination," said Crown Counsel.

"You may go now," said the judge to Ol Antoine.

On hearing the translation Ol Antoine stood and looked about him, as though wondering

137

who had called. The corporal came up and touched his elbow. "Come on, old-timer," he said, and led him away from the box.

"Just a moment," said the judge. "Mr. Edwards, would you please make arrangements to have this witness taken back to his Reserve, or as near to his Reserve as a car may reach? One of the police cars can be used."

"Milord, that is two hundred miles from here," said Crown Counsel.

"Exactly."

"With respect, My Lord, it would be unprecedented for the Crown to order police cars out on this errand."

"How fortunate for you," said the judge. "You are in a position of setting a precedent." And then with the current of his emotion breaking through in the way that so often brought him rebukes from Court of Appeal, he said, "The law brought him here, the law can take him home."

"I bow to Your Lordship's ruling."

"You're shmart man, chutch," said Ol Antoine.

"We will adjourn until two, for final argument," said His Lordship quickly.

Samuels and Edwards left the courtroom together.

"You're a fortunate man, Samuels."

"Don't make fun of me, please. It's my first murder case."

"I'm not making fun of you, I'm congratulating you. I had a perfectly solid case, and in just twenty minutes you took that jury away from me."

"I still think you're making fun of me."

"I don't know what to make of some of you young lawyers nowadays. I can't tell if you're geniuses or idiots. Samuels, a Cariboo jury will never permit the facts to influence its judgment. By nine o'clock tonight at the latest, and I don't think it will take that long — they'll probably deliberate just long enough to eat one more chicken dinner—they will have decided that that bloody-minded murderer of yours is guilty only of manslaughter. Or of some idiotic fancy that may occur to them. Guilty of picking up with intent to steal, possibly."

Crown Counsel swung his purple QC bag at the dusty floor of the corridor, watched its pendulum-swing, and continued, "Then, no doubt, our learned judge will fine that drunk ten dollars for fighting with intent to commit contempt of court, and another Assizes will have ended in the usual futility. Join me for lunch?"

"I'll be busy," said Samuels.

There was a lahelle game at the Indian camp on the stampede grounds as Ol Antoine approached and the chant of the gamblers fell pleasantly upon his ear. He had declined the offer of a ride in the police car and had gladly accepted instead a twenty-dollar bill, supplied from the pocket of Crown Counsel. Twenty dollars was a great deal of money, clearly enough to take care of the future in all foreseeable directions. The thunderstorm having passed over, he now intended to sit on the sidehill by himself, just within sound of the gambling song, and there think about what his speech had been like. He felt that the speech had gone very well. Possibly he would repeat some of it to himself. Tonight or perhaps tomorrow he would find Smith and ride back to Namko in Smith's truck.

He felt vaguely uneasy about Smith because there had been that fight in the courtroom. In his lifetime he had seen many fights, of course. Indian women usually fought by pulling hair and scratching, Indian men by wrestling and head-banging and gouging, and whites with their fists, and often all styles got mixed up together. Fights were part of the natural order of things. Prairie chicken liked to dance in the early spring, men liked to fight occasionally. It was true that Father O'Shay, the Oblate missionary, used to scold the people for fighting when he visited Namko Reserve. However, among the thoughts that his many years had given him time to examine, Ol Antoine sometimes considered matters of religion and he had come to the conclusion that God was not very much interested in fist-fights, one way or the other. The law, however, might be less tolerant than the Almighty and it was possible that Smith was in some trouble.

140

"Who was that drunk?" said the judge to the corporal, as they were finishing a T-bone steak at the restaurant. They had gone on duck-shooting expeditions many times when their professions brought them into contact on the northern coast and the corporal was one of the judge's favourite people.

"There's no identification on him," said the corporal. "He had eighty dollars loose in one pocket and a ten-dollar bill in another pocket and not another thing."

"And all the money will shortly be translated into liquor," said the judge, "as if he hadn't had enough already."

"He fought awfully hard for a drunk."

"Yes. Disgraceful. There is a type of beer-parlour cowboy in this town who is the white savage of this country."

"Somehow he doesn't seem like a beer-parlour cowboy to me," said the corporal.

"He is, believe me."

"Do you know him, then? He still won't talk to us, even to tell us his name."

"I have reason to know that he is a beer-parlour cowboy."

"Well, we'll make some checks and find out who he is quickly enough."

"Don't bother," said the judge. "Bring him up to me after the verdict is in tonight and I'll fine him under whatever name he chooses to use. The more speedily the matter is disposed of the better. I'm afraid it won't do much good, anyway. However, make sure he's sober."

"I'm not sure he was drunk," said the corporal. "There was a bit of a smell of beer on his shirt, but somehow he didn't seem like a drunk."

"He was a drunk," said the judge. "Let's consider more pleasant prospects. Wasn't that old Indian a treat?"

"That," said the corporal, "is a story for your book, Judge. Do you know, while everybody was looking for him he was down in our cells all the time?"

"No!"

"Yes, and under the wrong name. He'd been convicted by mistake in magistrate's court and was sitting out a five-day sentence down there. I never noticed him. One of the other men had locked him up there and I'd been too busy to be bothered about some drunk named Abraham. I almost fell down when one of the constables cottoned on to what had happened and told me about it."

"Well, nothing in the realm of court work is too strange to be believed," said the judge, making a mental note of the thing for his memoirs.

"Somebody finally paid his fine this morning and that's how he got up to the court in time," said the corporal.

"Who paid it, a white or an Indian?"

"McGuire didn't say."

"Well, I suppose that's a matter of no importance anyway. The hour is nearing two, Bill.

142

Shall we go?" The judge put fifteen per cent of the bill, precisely, beneath his plate and regretfully quenched his cigar. The cigar being only half-finished, he put the rest in his lower vest pocket.

The Jury

Samuels went to the courthouse that afternoon with hope and even a trace of confidence. By introducing a defence witness he had forfeited the favoured position of being the second man to address the jury. Nevertheless, he now felt that circumstance at last had favoured him.

During his despair of the day before, when Ol Antoine could not be found, Samuels had sought refuge in work. Any kind of work. From court adjournment until dawn, at which time he had snatched one hour of sleep, he had laboured over an address to the jury that dealt with Indian rights. Failing all else, he thought, he could lead them away from that overwhelming body of evidence by talking about Indian rights—up to the point at which his opponent would make justifiable protest.

Samuels had a friend in town, his only one up to that day. This friend was a doctor whose avocation was study of the Indian rights question in Canada. Samuels spent that night in the doctor's library. He read the Royal Proclamation of 1763, the federal parliamentary proceedings on the B.C. Indian Lands Question, the

144

briefs of the Allied Tribes of B.C. made during the 1920s, the Norris Judgment, the Sissons Judgments in the Northwest Territories. He had also drawn upon his own recollections of the noble red man as portrayed in *Hiawatha*. He had typed out twenty single-spaced folios of foolscap from which he intended to read to the jurymen. Now, after the Chief Joseph speech, he saw that it fitted as neatly as a duck's foot in fresh cowflap.

This would be the high ringing call for natural justice, the first trumpet blast of a new battle on the land rights question, the start of a new crusade.

But when he finally stood before those twelve solemn men of the jury he knew that he would never take the land rights question to the Supreme Court of Canada. Some brilliant lawyer would, some day, but it would not be Herman Samuels. He recognized his twenty-folio address for what it was—dreadful, fustian stuff, a pyramid of poop. He turned his twenty folios upside down on the counsel table and he walked away from them.

Instead of talking about Indian rights, he began talking about himself.

He was a very ordinary man, he said, like the members of the jury, like his client Gabriel, and sometimes he was dismayed by his own slowness of wit and sometimes he sinned, even as other ordinary men. He said he wished he were a much cleverer man because he was defending a fellow man who was on trial for his life, but all he could do, he said, was to make the best use he could of the brains God had given him, even though life was dear to all men, even the poorest and most ragged of men, and once taken could never be given back.

He persisted in that direction until he judged that Crown Counsel was just about to rise to protest that considerations of mercy were for authorities outside this court. Samuels then said that of course considerations of mercy were for authorities outside this court. He spoke almost in deprecation of the quality of mercy. The country could not function if only sentiment ruled, he said, and the men of the jury were men of the world and they knew this to be true.

Now, as good, common-sense men, they were to weigh the life of Gabriel Jimmyboy against the value of all the mass of evidence that the Government of Canada had collected and stored in its vaults these many months. It was an odd thing, wasn't it, that in matters such as this, no expense was too great for the Canadian taxpayer. In the late thirties, when Gabriel might have got some schooling, the Canadian taxpayer could afford only forty-three cents a day with which to house, clothe, feed and pay teachers for an Indian child in a residential school. But now, if the law be offended, no expense was too great. Well, that was the way the country had to be operated. The gentlemen of the jury realized that as a result of their own business experience with governments, and it was a thing that all sensible men should accept.

When he sensed that the jury was waiting for him to talk about Gabriel's life in the woods and how his client had felt while he was running from the vast power of the law, Samuels instead wound up his presentation in a few crisp sentences that dealt with the lack of eye witnesses and the danger of accepting even a great mass of circumstantial evidence. Then he sat down, leaving the jury thinking about many things that he had not said in that final address. They were still thinking about these things when Crown Counsel went into a long and somewhat tiresome examination of the details of the technical evidence.

Some of the jury ordered chicken again that night but many had turkey, knowing it would be their last meal on the Queen. They discussed the case as any normal group of men would. Did Gabriel look like a man who would murder (yes), had he done it a second time (no), and was there any point in hanging him? Then they got off on the side trails. Ol Antoine's testimony was discussed at length. The vote was eight to two, with two abstaining, that he had not been with Joseph but had heard the speech somewhere and memorized it, a remarkable feat and one of which he could be justly proud. There was much discussion of similar Indians known to jury members in years past, and many inter-

147

esting stories about them were told, some true. The Nez Percé horses were discussed and the whole tribe highly praised. After this there was brief discussion of the Chilcotin war of '64.

The judge was viewed favourably and the sheriff neutrally. Two jurors made pointed remarks about Crown Counsel because he had harped so much upon the fact that Ol Antoine had not been subpoenaed. Any reasonable man should know, they said, that it would make no difference whether you served an old Indian like that with a paper or not, he would still get there in Indian time. They felt that Crown Counsel was not as smart as he thought he was.

Samuels was not rated highly for intellect but won a twelve-to-nothing decision for honesty and two ranchers said they planned to give him their business because they preferred honest lawyers to smart ones.

Several felt that Samuels should have talked more about the Indians' situation in the Cariboo. True, many of them were loafers and worse, but they had had kind of a bad deal and it wasn't all their fault.

When supper had been cleared away the foreman said they should really make up their minds about this man Gabriel now. It was getting late and surely they'd heard everything said that there was to be said. The general feeling was that a manslaughter verdict would be appropriate, but then one of them said, "Well, what the hell. He said he was sorry." There is no record inside or outside court records of Gabriel's ever having made this statement. Haines was dead and how can you feel sorry for a dead man? But fiction proved more durable than fact. Years later members of this jury would say with the fine flavour of recollection in their mouths that they had acquitted Gabriel Jimmyboy because he had said he was sorry.

One or two thought that an acquittal might be weak in law, but one man declared that after all there was all that evidence of drinking.

In fact, there had been scarcely any such evidence. Police witnesses had merely noted that a couple of empty whisky bottles were in the cabin with Haines' body. But other members of the jury seemed to recollect hearing that this Indian had not drawn a sober breath for six months before the murder.

At eight-thirty P.M. they filed into the courtroom and declared that they found the accused not guilty because he had been too drunk to know what he was doing. The judge dismissed them with formal thanks. Thus does Canadian justice, blind, stupid and stumbling as she may sometimes seem, hit upon the truth more often than not.

Next it was Smith's turn.

The Corporal, and the
Blind Bitch Goddess
of Justice

He had then been caged for nine hours, during which he had refused food, refused drink and refused to wash the blood off his face. He had had some time to think, too. He had come to the conclusion that it was a lousy damn system. He was fed up with clerks in government offices who didn't look up when a taxpayer came in and he was fed up with beer-parlour bouncers, and the sooner he shook the dust of this damn town off his boots the happier he was going to be. As for Ol Antoine, the horse, that cultus bastard Walter Charlie, his mind dodged the subject entirely. He had a headache, too. And he was in no mood to listen to any police corporal yap at him. He disliked policemen at any time, but particularly now.

"We have got to go up there now and you still haven't washed the blood off your face," the corporal said. "Now why don't you spruce yourself up some before you go in front of the judge?"

There was silence.

"Because, take my word for it, if you go in front of the judge sulky like you are, he is likely to throw the book at you. I know that man. He's a friend of mine. We used to go duck-shooting together. And he has got the idea that you are just another beer-parlour cowboy."

Silence.

"Personally, I don't think you are. Your hands are too hard. You strike me as a working man. But you'd better convince the judge of it and in a hurry, too."

The corporal looked up to see Gabriel Jimmy-boy standing in the corridor of the gate of Smith's cell. "What's the matter, Gabriel? You're not homesick, are you? You don't live here any more, you know."

"I come get that sweater I leave," said Gabriel.

"Oh yes, that sweater. Well, your old cell door's open. Just help yourself. Say, do you know this man, Gabriel?"

"Might be it's Smith," said Gabriel.

"Yes, John Smith, no doubt. Or just J. Smith, maybe. Do you know him?"

Gabriel looked at Smith's bloody face. To the corporal it seemed expressionless but Gabriel thought he read there a shake of the head. "I guess I don't know that fella," said Gabriel.

"Ah, you joker," said the corporal. "Go pick up your sweater, Gabriel. Go and sin no more. Remember," he added, as Gabriel walked away, "you keep off the old sauce now, Gabriel."

151

"The judge is waiting," he said to Smith. "I say this to you once more. For your own good. Don't go up there sulky. I am trying to help you. Can you understand that? After all, I'm the man you kneed in the family jewels, and I am trying to help you."

Smith turned his head to look at the man for the first time. "Why don't you try just minding your own business?" he said.

"All right, if that's the way it is. Now we are going up there. You can go up in two ways. You can walk up, like a white man, or I can bring the constable in here and we'll throw the irons on you and drag you up. It is a long time since I had to handcuff a prisoner, but if I have to, I will do it."

Smith stood up. "Let's go upstairs," he said.

The corporal wrote J. Smith on the charge sheet and Smith shook his head when asked if he wanted a lawyer. All the spectators and the jurymen and the lawyers of the day were gone. The sky was dark outside the windows and the street below bright with neon and humming with the voices of many people intent on better things than courts.

"I am asking you once again," said the judge, "have you any explanation to offer for your disgraceful exhibition in this courtroom?"

"Nope."

"Address the judge as Your Lordship," said the corporal.

"Did you have a grudge against this man Walter Charlie whom you attacked here?" said the judge.

"I guess you'd call it that."

"I am enquiring as to what you call it. Did this explosion of your temper have anything to do with the case being heard, or was it simply a grudge, aided by alcohol?"

"It would be simplest to say it was just a grudge. I always hated his guts."

"And finding him in here, in my courtroom, you chose to engage in a brawl?"

"That's about it."

"I do not wish to know if that is 'about it.' Are those precisely the facts of the case?"

"Yep," said Smith.

What was the point, thought His Lordship, of seeking to impress the dignity of law upon a white savage. Also, he was weary. The Assizes had been long. He thought with pleasure of the crisp white sheets of his bed at the hotel and a book to sleep upon. He wrote what was to be the last entry of these Assizes on the big book in front of him, letting his tired voice flow past the moving pen.

"For contempt of this court there will be a fine of fifty dollars or, in default, thirty days imprisonment."

"Is that all?" said Smith, as the corporal tugged at his elbow to take him out.

The judge mistook his meaning. "Yes," he said. "That is all."

153

"Because," said Smith, "it happens I have got fifty bucks right here in my ass pocket, and I would say it was worth it."

"Come out, come out," said the corporal, pulling him towards the door.

The judge appeared to have failed to hear Smith's words. He was bent over his book again, writing. As the two men reached the door he said, "Just a moment, please." Then, continuing to write, he said in an even voice, "For a further contempt of this court there will be an additional penalty of sixty days imprisonment, without option of fine." Looking up he added loudly, harshly, "Possibly you have that in your ass pocket, also." The last few words no sooner left his mouth than he regretted them, as he always did when his impulses proved too strong for the sober tradition of his profession, and he compounded his error by saying, "No need to record that last remark, Mr. Stenographer, merely an aside, an aside."

The judge's dismay passed unnoticed by Smith, who staggered as his long-lost sanity returned with a rush to the pit of his empty stomach. "Two months, Judge!" he said, "Two months in jail, in haying time?"

"I warned you," said the corporal, under his voice.

"That's a little bit rough, Judge," said Smith.

"Remove the prisoner," said the judge.

"I'm beat," said Smith to himself, aloud. "I'm beat. Two months in jail, at this time of year."

"My Lord," said the corporal, "may I speak in this matter?"

The judge could scarcely have been more surprised if addressed by the photograph of Sir John French that hung in the outer hall, but his face remained impassive.

"Yes, Corporal."

"If Your Lordship pleases, I am not well acquainted with the prisoner but have observed him, over a period of time, and although he is not a very articulate person, I feel that he is genuinely sorry for his actions."

The judge looked long at the corporal. The ceiling light reflected two sharp shafts of light in his eyeglasses. When he spoke his voice was cold.

"Yours is a curious statement, Corporal. A period of time. A period of time might be an extremely short time. It might be nothing more than a few hours."

The corporal felt a hot blush rising from his collar. This time he had gone too far. He had presumed too much upon friendship. He had forgotten that between him and the judge existed a barrier never to be crossed, and he knew that that barrier would be made higher hereafter. He would always regret what he had lost this day because he liked the man.

"My Lord . . ."

The judge held up one hand. "I did not ask for a reply to that observation. You have known the prisoner for a period of time. That statement is clear and I accept it as sufficient. Prisoner . . ."

"Say 'Yes, My Lord,' " whispered the corporal.

"Yes, My Lord," said Smith.

"You seemed considerably disturbed by the jail sentence imposed upon you."

"It's kind of a rough sentence, Judge. In hay time."

"I suspect that more of your time is spent in beer parlours than in hay fields. There might come a day, prisoner—I doubt it, but there might come a day—when you will be operating a ranch yourself. If that time should come you will discover that hay is more than a matter of extra seasonal wages."

"Say 'Yes, My Lord,' " said the corporal.

"Yes, My Lord," said Smith.

The judge looked at him for a long time, long enough to twist a cigarette or kill a moose or sign a deed. "I shall go this far with you. This far, and no further. I am prepared to recommend to the Attorney-General that you spend your sentence in one of the open institutions. Perhaps in a forestry camp somewhere."

"As I see it," said Smith, "that just means that instead of sitting in jail I spend my two months cutting down pulp trees."

The judge's irritability returned. "It will improve your muscle tone, if not your disposition," he said. "Please remove the prisoner."

Smith and the corporal left, Smith saying, "Oh, she is rough, rough, rough."

All his penitence had been wasted. Had he remained stubborn to the end, he might have kept the satisfaction of knowing that he'd told the rest of the world that Smith didn't give a damn for it. Instead he had crawled, and he had gained nothing, because he was still out of circulation for two whole months, and even his guiding contracts for the American hunters would have to be given away to a neighbour.

Norah, Again

❧

Norah did not see Ol Antoine come into the yard and enter the house, where the baby was sleeping. She was milking the Guernsey cow. Sherwood and Roosevelt had been weaned to the thin blue milk of wild Hereford Grade range cows, but for both Exeter and John they kept the Guernsey.

Smith despised dairy cows and he would not by word or deed admit that this one existed. Soon he would be suggesting again that canned milk was quite good enough for children, that is, as long as children really needed milk at all. She knew he looked forward to the day when he would butcher this Guernsey or sell, trade or give her to some other rancher less fastidious than Smith about the quality of his stock. In fact, Smith was not truly enamoured of the Herefords, on which his income depended and for whose nourishment and care this ranch was supposed to operate. Once, at a stampede dance, Norah had heard him complain to his peers that keeping Herefords was a losing game. "The bastards breed like flies, you know," he had said. Many had laughed, but she had been furious.

She knew the words were only partly said in jest.

Why wasn't he back yet, damn him? When she came into the house Ol Antoine was sitting beside the stove. He always sat beside stoves, even when the stove was cold, even when the day was hotter than the hinges on the gates of hell.

This was such a day. There had been a frost three nights before. The first touch of yellow had appeared on the poplar groves. Soon all the lovely trees would be carrying millions of golden coins upon their boughs. But then the heat had returned. Coming from the bouncing sunlight of the dusty yard into the half-night of the house, it was not surprising that she failed to see Ol Antoine curled up, as he was, like a piece of dry old bacon rind.

She smelt him almost as quickly as she saw him, the smoky, stale-meat scent of Indian.

"Ol Antoine!" she said. "Are you ever a sight for sore eyes!"

He was so astonished he started talking in Chilcotin.

"You came in with Smith, I spose?"

He kept on talking to himself.

"I said, I spose Smith is here at last, is he?"

"Awful waum," said Ol Antoine. "Waum illa-hie."

She sighed. It was still a man's world, even for a sexless old stick like this.

"It is hot," she said. "I got some lime juice made, Ol Antoine. You have some. It's good in the heat."

159

She got the quart sealer that was wrapped in the wet cloth for cooling, ice being a luxury unknown in summer, and she poured some of the pale, sour liquid into the peanut butter jar that had the big handle on it, and she put it into his little withered hand.

"I guess it was a real interesting trial, Ol Antoine. But I don't hear anything about it. My radio's broke still, and I don't know anything that went on."

He considered this. "Funny thing," he said, "they don't hang that fella Kapriel. That chutch lets him go."

"Well, that's nice."

"Might be Kapriel comes here for hay," said Ol Antoine.

"Oh! Oh. Well, Ol Antoine, he must not bring any whisky here. If he brings any whisky I will run him off the place—Smith will run him off."

"He kets little trunk with that Walter Charlie when he's out of that chail, but he don't drink here, I don't think."

"Did you come in with Smith in the truck?"

"Good year for hay, I think. That grass is sure good. Lots Intian peoples come make hay for Smith this year, I think."

"Yes, the weather is nice, isn't it? Nice weather. Smith is with you, Ol Antoine? You come in his truck from Williams Lake?"

"Smith he's shmart man."

"Ol Antwyne," she said, "where is Smith? I

can't run this ranch by myself any longer." There was a break in her voice.

He sighed. "Smith gives me paper for you," he said. She waited. "I don't know what that paper he says," said Ol Antoine. "I want to ket somepoty read that paper to me, but I forket." He sighed again. "I get old, and I forket things."

"Well, you don't have to apologize for not reading my mail. Oh, never mind, never mind, old man. Just give me the paper." She held out her hand, but he made no move to pass it to her.

"I break that quarter horse he's kot," he said. "I do it real quick. I do it right now." And then, to reinforce the immediacy of what he said with another word that meant much the same thing to him, he added, "Might be I shtart tomorrow."

"I don't care about the quarter horse," she said.

"I don't charge Smith for break that horse. I do it free. I do it for him free cultus potlach."

"I don't care about the horse, Ol Antoine."

"Him's good horse that. I *know*. I watch that horse, loooooong time I watch that horse."

"Give me the paper, Ol Antoine."

"I don't know what it says, that paper."

"Give me the paper and I will read it to you. I will read it out loud and you will know everything it says."

He pulled a piece of notepaper, many times folded, out of his breast pocket and passed it to her.

161

She read the first line to herself and then said, "Damn him! The little turd!"

Ol Antoine felt quite sure that the paper did not say this. He put his head closer. Since she had promised, she read it aloud.

"Dear Norah, I will be a little bit hard to get hold of for a while. (*As if he was ever any other way*, she said.) The Indians are all contracted and will get the hay up okay but you may have to keep Sherwood and Roosevelt back from school for the first month. The Indians will work okay. They had a big stick game here and as usual it ended up with nobody winning and everybody losing so everybody is now broke. I have noticed that being broke is a big help to an Indian in his thinking."

"Sure was goot kame," Ol Antoine agreed. "Three tays that kame."

She read some more. "You had better send Sherwood or Roosevelt out to kill us a moose as I imagine meat stock is low. Tell them they are to kill a dry cow or else a paddle bull. Nothing else. No old bull. Paddle bull or dry cow. Pass my American hunters along to Frenchie, he's got a class A guide's licence."

She dropped the hand that held the paper. "And that's it. Where in the name of God is he, Ol Antoine?"

"Ent nothing more she says, that paper?"

She found some more writing on the other side of the sheet of stiff paper, which had been borrowed from the court clerk's office at

162

Williams Lake, she noted. Her expression changed as she read this.

"Well," she said, "did you know about this, old man?"

He was sipping his lime juice. He drank as Smith drank, tiny sips, holding the liquid in his mouth before letting it slip down his throat.

"Well," Norah said, "well, I spose the boys and me can handle the hay and the crews. The weather looks good. We can manage, I guess. Maybe it all amounts to the turn of the Smith luck. He never told you about this, Ol Antwyne?"

This time he looked at the paper that he could not read and she read it aloud to him. "I have landed a two-month government contract cutting pulpwood. Do not worry. All is well. Smith."

Their tamest Whisky Jack flew in the door she had left open. Norah held out a scrap of meat from the table and with a moth-like flutter of his wings he came over, took it from her hands and rushed out into the sunlight. She smiled. It was a pity she did not smile more often, for it was a nice smile. "Things are never as bad as we think they are, Ol Antwyne," she said.

"Shmart man, Smith," he said, "awful shmart man."

And the Horse

Of course, she was bound to find out what happened, sooner or later, and she did. There was quite a bit of action in the Smith house when he finally came home. She was a hurricane on a ten-cent piece that day.

But the hay was good that summer. Beef went up in the fall, and the young banker came down to earth. It was an open winter, too. They didn't have to start feeding until February and they were able to turn the stock out on spring range a mere two months later. They were still broke, of course, but they were still there.

However, when another summer came around, Ol Antoine still had not talked to that quarter horse. So one day Smith buckled on his old workaday sunset rowel spurs and climbed aboard that quarter horse and bucked him out in the usual way. He turned out to be just another horse.

Also by Paul St. Pierre
Smith and Other Events
Chilcotin Holiday
Sister Balonika
Boss of the Namko Drive
British Columbia — Our Land